Praise for Cliff Jacobson and
Justin Cody's Race to Survival

"Dear Cliff Jacobson, I started your book a day or two ago and I am
almost done. I haven't been able to take my eyes off of it. I don't
usually read a ton, but I have sat down for hours. And just by the
way, I am being completely honest."

—*Joey Sullivan, age 13*

"I have recently downloaded your new book and I have really
enjoyed reading it. I have recently been hired as a reading
intervention teacher and I would like to use this book in my
classroom. Thanks so much for offering this book, I anticipate it to
be a big hit among my middle school students!"

—*Bob Stein*

"This is so fascinating, so promising, Cliff. I always believed you
had tremendous writing skills in other venues as well. You have the
varied background of experiences to write many fascinating
accounts which also convey those human social values and insights
so badly needed in our youth today."

—*Bernie Bast*

"Cliff, I just read your book about Justin Cody. Nicely done. I've
been paddling for 50 years and it is probably the most concise
writing on basic woodcraft. I enjoyed it."

—*Jay Hanks*

D1596809

JUSTIN CODY'S RACE TO SURVIVAL
High Adventure in the Canadian Wilderness

Cliff Jacobson

10,000 Lakes Publishing
Chaska, Minnesota

Cliff Jacobson

2023

First digital edition, 2017, ISBN: 978-1-64007-788-1
First print edition, 2019, ISBN: 978-0-9974768-3-5

Editing by Colton Witte and Sean Bloomfield
Formatting by Beth Hercules
Cover Design by Melvyn Paulino

For signed copies visit CliffCanoe.com

For wholesale information visit 10kLP.com

ACKNOWLEDGMENTS

A big thanks to the following people who kindly read the manuscript and offered advice, photos or illustrations: Carol Bradford (three illustrations), Darrell Foss, Sue Harings, Clarissa Jacobson, Jim and Grace Mandel, Larry Rice, Darlene Patterson, Larry Rice and Bob Tucker.

-Cliff

SYNOPSIS

Thirteen-year-old Justin Cody is failing two classes and is addicted to texting and video games. Forced to take a wilderness canoe trip in Canada with his Grandpa Henry, Justin is thrust into a race for survival when the two discover a stolen top-secret drone developed by the U.S. Military. Grandpa Henry is kidnapped, and Justin—who knows nothing about canoeing and camping—must journey alone to a distant lake that promises rescue.

Race to Survival is a high adventure tale and wilderness skills book in one! Young readers will be entertained while they learn practical outdoor skills. Lessons include how to read a map and compass, make fire when the forests are wet with rain, rig a stormproof camp, what to do when you're caught in a lightning storm, tips to repel mosquitoes and black flies, important knots, essentials for a stay in the woods, emergency signals, wild foods that you can easily find and safely identify, what to do if you meet a bear or cow moose while you're hiking, and many more! Essentially, this is a "canoeing-camping-survival" how-to book dressed in riveting fictional clothes, most of which based upon real-life experiences. There are also four appendices and dozens of informational side-bars—a first for books of this type.

TABLE OF CONTENTS

The Plan

CHAPTER 1 — THE PLAN

Thirteen-year-old Justin Cody stared at the huge waterfall below him. He marveled at the power of the rushing water and how it swirled around the rocks below, sending showers of rainbow-colored droplets skyward. As his grandpa would say, "This one's a *must* portage," meaning they would have to carry their canoe and gear around it. An old trail that was choked with bushes skirted the falls, and Justin knew they'd have taken it if his grandpa was here. But his grandpa was gone—he had flown away an hour ago. In all of his young life, he had never been so alone. As far as he could see, all he could see were rocks and trees, trees and rocks, and of course the river. There were no cars, no roads, no buildings, no human voices. Except for the swish of a light breeze and the determined hum of mosquitoes, his new world was silent.

He had so many questions. *Why did we have to find the damn flying saucer?* Yeah, a flying saucer. If they hadn't found it, Gramps would be here now, and they'd be canoeing down the river. *What's so important about it, anyway, and why did they send a float plane to fetch it?*

Most of all he wondered, *Why did Gramps yell "Run, Justin, run!" just before he flew away with those men, leaving him behind?* Justin was worried about Gramps, but he was also confused. *Did the men kidnap Grandpa? Why didn't they chase me?* Instead they just closed the door and flew away without saying a word. Maybe Gramps was just warning him to get out of the way of the propeller, or maybe Gramps was so fed up with him that he wanted to leave him there.

Today was the fourth day of their canoe trip and Justin had resisted every minute of it. He balked when asked to do simple chores. He didn't want to fetch water or gather firewood or wash the dishes after meals. He made it perfectly clear to Gramps that he absolutely, positively *did not* want to be here. Maybe he had crossed a line and his grandpa had had enough of him.

He wished he had his damn phone! He wanted to text Sara, his girlfriend—almost girlfriend. She was smart and would know what to do. He and Sara were in English class together and he couldn't take his eyes off her. She was so beautiful and so nice. They were constantly texting back and forth at school, and sometimes after school, they'd game together on his Xbox. Though they were opposites in some ways, they were best friends, too. That was all—at least that was how Sara saw it—but Justin wanted to be more.

Sara never got into trouble, he always got into trouble! She was the clever one, he a klutz. He often got caught when he played on his phone, but she never got caught. And unlike him, Sara was a really good student, getting A's and B's in all her classes. She said school was easy if you just paid attention when the teacher taught important things, the rest of the time you could do what you wanted. Justin once asked her how she knew what was important and what wasn't. "I don't know how, I just know," she replied. Anyway, once school was out Sara would fly to Cape Cod for the summer to be with her aunt. Justin wouldn't see her again until fall.

Justin knew that his parents and teachers were fed up with him playing on his cell phone in class. They had taken it away from him more times than anyone could count, but somehow, he had always found a way to sneak it back. Once he got into big trouble when a teacher took the phone away and locked it in his desk. Justin knew where the teacher kept the key, so between classes, he unlocked the desk and replaced the phone with an old flip-phone he had. It looked different than his smart phone, but he was sure the teacher wouldn't notice. *Wrong!* When Justin's mom discovered what he had done, she brought the roof down on him! She said he was grounded for life. No phone, no Xbox, no nothing! Justin was flunking and no one knew what to do.

He wasn't a bad kid, never mean or hurtful, and he never talked back to his teachers. But he wouldn't pay attention in class or do his homework. The one thing he did well—quite well—were puzzles. In fact, he was the only kid in math class who could solve a Rubik's Cube. His math teacher thought he was pretty smart, that he could get A's if he would just apply himself. He needed what the teacher called an "attitude adjustment."

Justin had failed two classes—social studies and English—enough to land him in summer school. But neither his parents nor his teachers thought that six more weeks of sitting in a hot classroom would improve his grades or his attitude. So together they came up with a brainy idea. Justin's Grandpa Henry, who was a nationally known wilderness expert, thought it was brilliant. Henry agreed to take Justin on a wilderness canoe trip—that is, if Justin agreed to go. They would be spending a month in Canada, and Justin would keep a daily journal, take pictures of the trip, and afterwards, write a report about it. In return, his teachers would pass him in English and social studies, and he wouldn't have to go to summer school.

Henry Jansen was well known in the outdoor field. He had written more than a dozen books about canoeing and camping. Heck, Justin even had an autographed copy of one of them, though he'd never read it. Henry never gamed or texted, and apparently, he hated music because there wasn't a single song on his smart phone. His computer was nearly a decade old and he didn't own a tablet. But he loved a good time and would often stay up all night partying with Justin's mom and her friends. He looked young, no one could believe he was 75.

Justin's mom and grandpa hoped that some time away from texting and gaming on a long wilderness canoe trip would cure him of his addiction to them and teach him the value of learning. Henry had chosen what he called a "mildly challenging" river in northern Canada, one he had done three times before. He said the river had lots of canoeable rapids—meaning ones that were safe to paddle, if you knew what you were doing—and beautiful waterfalls, large lakes, awesome fishing, and long **eskers** that were great for camping. He said they might even see some moose or caribou, and maybe bears too, though he didn't consider them a problem.

*An **esker** is a long, winding ridge that is made up of sand and gravel that was left behind when the ice from a glacier melted thousands of years ago. The shorelines of northern rivers are often crowded with bushes, so there's not much room to pitch a tent; eskers have lots of open space so they're great for camping. Some eskers stretch for miles!*

"The river is very remote," said Henry. "Only a few parties canoe it each year, most in late July or early August. We'll go in June, so it's doubtful we'll see a soul. It can be chilly that time of year, so good wool clothes and rain gear are important. There are no roads to the river, so we'll have to use a float plane to get in and out." *Quite an adventure!* "Justin will learn to focus on small but important things, like how to tie a knot that won't slip and how to waterproof his gear, so it won't get wet in rain or a capsize. He'll discover that there are serious consequences for doing things wrong on a canoe trip and that a smart-aleck attitude just makes things worse."

As they planned, he hugged Justin's mom reassuringly and said, "Don't worry, honey, I won't let anything bad happen to him." He added that he was bringing a satellite phone, but it was for emergencies only. He would not waste battery life making casual calls, and he would not be checking the phone for messages.

Justin had been camping once before—when he was eight, Gramps took him on a week-long canoe trip into the Boundary Waters Canoe Area of Minnesota. They paddled a canoe, camped in a tent, portaged heavy packs on rough trails through the woods, and built big campfires each night. They also caught fish—Gramps said they were Walleyes—and they tasted amazing! But so what?

When they presented Justin with the option of going with Henry, he thought back to their B.W.C.A. trip. A week in the woods with Gramps was fine, *for a kid,* but now he was 13, and the thought of eating freeze-dried food from plastic bags sucked. No Big Macs or pizza, battling bugs and rain. Worst of all, there was no electricity. Running water was when he ran down to the lake after it! Same thing every day—paddle and camp, camp and paddle, then paddle and camp some more—*how boring!* Thirty days with no phone, no TV, no Xbox—*forget it!* Tantrum time.

"I'm not going! I'm not going!" he screamed at his mother.

"Fine. Summer school starts in two weeks," she offered.

"No, no, no!" he yelled as he ran to his room and slammed the door.

For a while, he just sat on the bed and stared at his wall—his completely blank wall. He felt miserable and empty. When he'd calmed down, he began to weigh his choices. Six weeks of summer school or four weeks canoeing with Gramps? Six versus four, four versus six. Summer school would be awful, even more awful than camping out and eating bad food. Either way, there would be no phone or games. At least while he was on the canoe trip his parents wouldn't be on his case.

Reluctantly, he decided to go.

CHAPTER 2 — THE POSSIBLES PACK

Justin was tired of staring at the river, tired of wondering what to do. He daydreamed about how he got into this mess—his thoughts returned to the clump of trees on the high hill where they had eaten lunch just hours before. There, they had stumbled upon a flying saucer! Grandpa said not to touch it—it could be a bomb. About the size of a car tire, it was too small to hold people. It had a bright red tail fin and a large exhaust port. Otherwise, it looked just like the flying saucers Justin had seen in movies.

The words USAF AERODRONE were printed on one side and SOLEIL 1 was written in cursive on the other. *Holy shit*, he thought. *It's a military drone!* The exhaust port was reflective, not black like a car's exhaust pipe. Grandpa said that whatever it burned, burned clean. The only imperfection was the bent big red tail fin. Gramps thought the fin must have bent on impact, or possibly been hit by a big bird, like a goose, while flying. Justin knew that birds had flown into airplane engines in the past and some of the planes had crashed. There were no sticks or dirt covering the drone, so it probably hadn't been there for very long.

USAF Aerodrone

For a long time, they studied the little saucer. They walked around it, but Gramps said not to touch it. Justin's dad had given him a new digital camera for the trip and Justin used it to photograph the drone from every angle. He even took some selfies of him and Gramps standing proudly by it. Gramps said that after lunch, he'd get out the satellite phone and call authorities. "They'll be thrilled we found it; this baby's probably pretty pricey. Heck, we might even get a reward!"

After a while, they grew tired of looking at the drone. It was past noon and they were hungry, so they strolled back to the canoe, where Gramps grabbed the possibles pack, which contained their lunch. Then they hiked to a high hill that had some shady trees and a good view of the waterfalls.

"We'll eat here," he said.

"Why's it called a **possibles pack**?" asked Justin.

Possibles Pack

"Because it contains everything we might possibly need for a day hike away from camp or an emergency night out in the woods. In the old days, every mountain man carried a possibles bag or pack. There might be flint and steel for making fire, a candle, fish line, extra gun flints, buffalo jerky or **pemmican**, rope, tin cup, tomahawk, etc. Every man had his own idea of what to bring. If we lost everything on our canoe trip, but we had the possibles pack, we could survive. When we camp tonight, I'll show you what's in there and how to use it." Justin nodded along before Gramps added, "By the way, if you had read the book I gave you before we left, you would know what's inside!"

Justin just rolled his eyes and mumbled, "Yeah, right, Gramps."

Gramps said nothing, looked away and shook his head.

Lunch was easy, and much the same every day. There was pita bread or whole wheat crackers, cheese and hard salami, peanut butter and jam, salty mixed nuts,

Pemmican was invented by the American Indians. It was made from dried buffalo, deer, or elk meat that was pounded into tiny pieces then mixed with melted fat, dried fruit and nuts. Pemmican was very nutritious, and it didn't spoil in the summer heat. It was the main food of the fur traders and Arctic explorers. A recipe for pemmican is in Appendix 3.

and always a Snickers bar. Leftovers went back into the possibles pack to be eaten tomorrow. Food was never wasted on a canoe trip!

Suddenly, Justin snapped out of his daydream. *Gramps is gone, sitting here won't change that,* he understood. He hoped the airplane would come back for him, and soon! *Gramps will see to that, won't he?* But he couldn't shake the thought that Gramps was mad and wanted to leave him. Well, he'd just have to get by on his own until Gramps returned. Right now, the important thing was to unpack the canoe and set up camp, then wait. Justin had learned some useful skills over the last four days with Gramps. He knew how to pitch the tent, cut wood, and make a fire. As long as he had food, he'd be okay. With fragile confidence, he ambled back to the small gravel beach above the falls where the canoe had been tied.

As he neared the beach something seemed off. Had he come out of the woods in a different spot? The canoe wasn't there. He walked a little way up shore in each direction, but the canoe was gone—gone! *Did it go over the falls!?* Every possibility crossed his mind but it having come lose was impossible! They had pulled it up on shore and Gramps had tied it to a tree—not with a normal knot, but with a **double half-hitch,** which Gramps said would never accidentally come loose. Still, it must have, because the canoe wasn't there! All the packs, all the food, the fishing gear—*everything*—was gone! *What should I do?* Justin's thoughts raced as his newfound confidence melted into panic. His legs went numb, so he sat down to think. He had to figure this out!

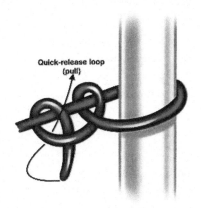

Quick-release loop (pull)

Double Half-Hitch

He wrapped his arms around his knees and began to rock back and forth, faster and faster! Maybe it would clear his mind. But it didn't, it just made him more afraid, so he stopped rocking and just sat quietly, his gazed ahead into space. After a short time, he slowly rose and screamed into the nothingness, "Damn, damn, damn! I hate you, Grandpa! I hate you!"

He had barely gotten the words out when he began to cry. *What if grandpa isn't coming back? Maybe he's dead and watching over him from the big campground in the sky.* Suddenly, he was ashamed at his outburst and he cried again. "Sorry, Gramps, sorry. I didn't mean it. Honest, I didn't mean it," he blurted between the tears. When he ran out of tears he sat down again, and for what seemed like a long time, just stared at the place where the canoe had been. Slowly, his mind began to clear.

The possibles pack! The thought of it hit him like a ton of bricks. Maybe it was still at the lunch spot. If so, he could survive, at least until the floatplane came back for him. With renewed hope, he raced back up the hill, hollering, "Please be there! Please be there!"

Yes! It was there, still sitting by the tree. Their lifejackets were on the ground nearby. It was getting chilly, so he put one on. Like Gramps, he often wore it in camp for warmth. Gramps' map and GPS were there too. He always brought them ashore at lunch stops to verify their position. Then he would call Justin over and show him where they were—like he was slyly trying to teach him how to read a map. At this, Justin would usually just roll his eyes, he thought he'd had plenty maps in social studies.

But strangely, he had been cooperative earlier today when Gramps showed him their position. He tapped a point on the map and said, "See this bar across the river that says *F*? *F* **stands for falls**—that's where we are!" Then he pointed to a place upstream where the river forked. "We took the right branch, which goes over this falls," his finger traced their path. "If we had gone left, there would be no falls—just a long rapid. See the short hash marks that cross the river here? Those indicate rapids. Notice that they continue for just over an inch on the map. On this map, 1.25 inches equals one mile, so the rapid is about a mile long."

"I know, I know," yelled Justin, "I know how maps work!"

"Okay, okay, but there's more," said Gramps. Justin sighed, but listened. Gramps continued, "There's an old saying, 'water seeks its own level,' which means that the rapid must drop the same amount as the falls."

"The falls drops 25 feet, so the rapid must also drop 25 feet. But the falls does it in a single plunge, whereas the rapids need a mile."

"Sounds easier to paddle than carry everything across a portage," Justin cut in unenthusiastically.

Gramps continued without much pause, "Canoeing a rapid with a 25 foot per mile drop isn't difficult, if you know what you're doing—but if you don't, you'll crash and burn!" He looked side-long at Justin to see if he had his attention. He didn't, and tried to excite Justin, nonetheless. "We came this way because you're still not very good in

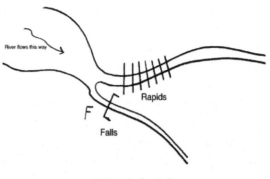

F Stands for Falls

rapids, but before we're done with this trip, you will be—and you'll be whooping and hollering all the way through the **rooster tails**!" On the plus side, this route choice was delightfully remote, as it's more fun to run rapids than to portage falls. They could probably camp here all summer and never see a soul.

"Cool," said Justin with a shrug.

Gramps was always studying the map, even though he had done the river three times before. He had marked all the waterfalls and

Rooster Tails are canoeing slang for big standing waves!

rapids, favorite fishing spots, campsites, and places where he had seen wildlife. He had also copied notes from previous parties who had run the river. He said that water levels change due to

rain and drought—that an easy rapid one year might be a killer the next and that many people have drowned canoeing rivers they had done before just because they thought they knew what was ahead. "You can never have too much information about a river," he said rhetorically. Justin wasn't convinced. Gramps had done the river three times. *Three times!* He said he knew it like the back of his hand. If so, why did he keep taking notes? *Old guy's going senile!*

Now Justin stared at the map. He regretted telling Gramps that he had learned about maps in school, when in truth he had been texting under his desk during the lessons. He worried that if Gramps didn't return, he would have to go alone to where the airplane was supposed to pick them up. He thought again about his smart-aleck attitude and how Gramps had tried to get him to read the book he had given him just before the trip. Now he wished he had read the book! But the milk was spilled, and there was no reason to cry over it.

With trembling hands, he opened the possibles pack. On top and neatly folded was the red and white checkered plastic tablecloth they set out at every meal. The huge black ants printed on the face always made him smile. The lunch leftovers were in a nylon bag below. There was cheese, salami, nuts, and half-full bottles of PB & J.

Also in the possibles pack were Grandpa's very sharp little Swedish hatchet, a stainless-steel **Sierra Cup**, a lightweight nylon tarp, complete with parachute cord and aluminum tent stakes, and a small tool kit containing epoxy glue, duct tape, a coil of light snare wire, needles and thread, a folded piece of heavy-duty aluminum foil, some diaper pins, a butane lighter, more parachute cord, a few Band-Aids, triple antibiotic

Sierra Cup

ointment and a small bottle of liquid soap.

Justin knew that there were big first-aid and repair kits in one of the packs in the canoe, what he had now were just emergency back-ups. Over and over, his grandpa had stressed the importance of backing up essentials. He called it "belt-and-suspenders" wisdom. "If your belt breaks and you're wearing suspenders, your pants won't fall down!" he said. The back-ups included a **space blanket**—it was silver on one side, red on the other, a giant black plastic bag, the 50-foot-long nylon rope they used every night when they set up camp, two freeze-dried meals that each served four, a plastic jar with about 25 bouillon cubes, a small bag of instant rice, and four energy bars.

Hooray, more food! Gramps had told Justin that every pack contained some food. He said he "spread good things around" so they wouldn't go hungry if they lost a pack in a capsize or to a bear. Beyond the food, his most exciting find was a waterproof plastic box that contained the satellite phone. He brightened instantly when he saw it and immediately tried to make a call. He pushed the start button and waited. Nothing happened. He pushed it again, but this time, he held it down for a while. Seconds later, a welcoming graphic appeared that showed how to extend and rotate the antenna. He followed the directions and the words *Registering* came on screen, followed by *Registered*.

Cool, he thought. *I'll just call Mom and get outta here!* He punched in his phone number and hit *Send*. There was a beep followed by an error message. He typed the number in again. Another error message. *Forgot to dial 1;* he tried again. No go. He tried

*A **space blanket** is a thin, lightweight blanket made from heat-reflective plastic. The silver side reflects body heat and should be placed against your skin. The blanket can also be spread out on the ground and used as a rescue signal. The silver-aluminum color flashes in the sun and the flashes can be seen a long way away by a rescue party.*

a dozen times without success. Frustrated, he turned off the phone and put it back into the box. He sat fuming, pissed at himself because on the first day of their trip Gramps had tried to show him how to use the satellite phone, but Justin wouldn't pay attention. He had just put his hands over his ears and walked away hollering, "I know, I know, I know how to use a damn phone, I'm not stupid!" He wished he had listened, but he was still confident that he would figure it out when he had more time.

Just when he thought he had exhausted the contents of the pack he discovered a zippered compartment behind the front panel. Sealed in a plastic bag was a book. Not the autographed book his grandpa had given him some time ago, but a bigger book. A much bigger book. On the cover, it said, *Everything You Could Want to Know About Canoeing and Camping.*

Well, he thought, *if Gramps doesn't come back, I'll have to read it!*

CHAPTER 3 — THE CHICAGO MAFIA

The International Finance Institute, or IFI, occupied the entire top floor of the posh Lincoln-Sheridan hotel in Chicago. The elevator required a special key to get there—you had to be invited to get in. The few hotel employees who had seen the inside of the IFI said that it was the most lavish suite in the hotel. The rooms had the finest furniture and linens. The floor was polished marble with expensive Persian rugs scattered about. Two ornate brass pillars and a milk-white marble bench guarded the huge glass door that marked the entrance to the suite. A sign on the door said Absolutely By Appointment Only in raised gold leaf lettering. When out-of-towners asked about the IFI, hotel staffers suppressed a smile and looked around suspiciously before answering. Then they would lean in close and whisper, "It's not a finance institute, it's a branch of the Mafia!"

Days before, in a far corner of a warmly lit room in the suite, a man in his twenties and of slight build was staring at a small red dot that was moving slowly across his computer screen. His task was to make sure the aerodrone arrived safely at its destination. This was his first big project and he couldn't screw it up. The aerodrone, named SOLEIL 1, was a miniature flying saucer, and a one-of-a-kind prototype developed by the U.S. Air Force.

It was special because it ran on water and used sunlight to split water molecules into hydrogen and oxygen, then it burned the hydrogen in the oxygen. The process was sort of like how plants photosynthesize—they use water, carbon-dioxide, and simple nutrients to make oxygen and food. The aerodrone was useful because it was amazingly powerful for its size, able to carry 20 pounds, enough for a small bomb!

It had two methods of propulsion, with a top speed of 650 mph on its hydrogen-rocket engine, or 150 mph on the solar-powered, retractable propellers, which it used mostly to hover. And perhaps most interesting was that the drone could re-fuel itself. When the water tank got low, it would just seek the nearest body of water, then swoop down and suck up fresh reserves with a snorkel. With hardly a delay it then continued on its way.

The military named it *Soleil*, French for sun, because it used energy from the sun to split the water. Its only exhaust was water vapor, which made it almost impossible to detect, especially with the latest stealth technology—it couldn't be tracked on traditional radar or thermal-imaging devices. In order to follow it, you had to decrypt the tracking data on its flight chip.

The man in the corner of the ISI smiled smugly at the ease with which he had cracked the code. It allowed Mafia operatives to steal the aerodrone from a military base in Massachusetts a month ago. Surprisingly, the press had been silent about the theft. It was so top secret that the military was all hushed up about it—they were probably too embarrassed to report it missing.

The mafia stole it when a wealthy buyer with bad intentions offered $30 million for it if it did what the military claimed—that it could fly across international borders undetected. But he wouldn't pay out until he saw a real-time test that proved it. That was what they were doing now—flying the aerodrone from Chicago to Anchorage, Alaska, a distance of about 4,000 miles and across two international borders—U.S. to Canada, then back into the U.S. It was in northern Canada right now and was going good so far. If it made it to Anchorage undetected, the deal was done.

Just then, a key turned in the door and an elderly man in an expensive suit entered the room with a much younger woman on his arm. They sprawled lazily down in an over-stuffed chair by the computer. The man held a cup of coffee in one hand and a thick cigar in the other. The woman snuggled tight against him but wasn't paying attention, instead texting and noisily chewing gum.

"Got a surprise for ya, Geek," said the man.

"Yeah, what?" came the reply.

"Roxy and me got married yesterday. Got me a hottie."

"Congratulations, Frank. You too, Roxy," said Geek, barely looking up from his computer. Roxy kept chewing and texting.

"Say something to Geek," said Frank, annoyed at the two of them.

Roxy looked up, forced a smile, and said, "Hi, Geek, what ya doin'?"

"Watching—uh—something," he replied.

"What's 'something'?" she asked.

"Enough!" the man cut in, "you know the rules, Roxy—beat it!"

As she rose to leave, he pressed a 100-dollar bill into her hand and instructed, "Honey, go down and buy yourself a cappuccino, I'll call ya when we're done." She smiled superficially, pecked him on the cheek, and silently walked out.

"Say, Geek, when do you think it'll hit Anchorage?" asked Frank.

"I've programmed it to re-fuel every 700 miles. It will have to occasionally divert from its flight path to find water, so that will slow its progress some. But if all goes well, I figure it should arrive in Anchorage sometime late tonight. I sent our boys the coordinates of the rendezvous this morning. I think you can go ahead and alert them to be ready to pick it up."

"Good job, Geek. Keep me informed," said Frank. He stood up, took a long drag on his cigar, and slowly shuffled towards the door. As he began to turn the doorknob, Geek stopped him.

"The drone—the drone, it's not blinking. It's not blinking!"

"Whadaya mean, it ain't blinking?" snapped Frank.

"I mean, it's not blinking! The red indicator stopped. Not blinking means it's down!"

"Down? Down where?! Find out where it's down! It's worth $30 million. That's *thirty* million dollars! Get me coordinates, Geek. Get me coordinates, *now!*"

Geek frantically tapped the keyboard, and seconds later, some numbers appeared in a corner of the computer screen.

"Got 'em, Frank. It's on a hill by a river in a remote part of Canada. Systems check reads 'good,' which means it should be able to fly. I can't tell what brought it down, but it sure wasn't lack of water, because it's damn-near surrounded! It appears undamaged, and it's nowhere near anybody—looks like the closest town is 300 miles away."

"Call Max in Anchorage and give him the new coordinates. Tell him to get a hold of Sam and that bush-pilot guy. Tell 'em they need to fly out *immediately* and get this thing. If there's anyone around who saw it go down, tell Max to do what's necessary, but make it look like an accident."

Geek nodded but didn't immediately act.

"Do you get me, Geek? Fix this!"

CHAPTER 4 — THE STORM

Back in the wilderness black clouds were building and the sky was getting darker. A storm was moving in. Justin checked the thermometer on the zipper pull of his jacket. It read 44 degrees, but he wasn't at all cold. He was dressed right for the weather—his grandpa had seen to that. He was wearing wool long underwear on top and bottom, thick wool socks, a checkered red wool jacket-shirt, nylon river pants, and a hooded Gore-Tex parka that came nearly to his knees, and of course, a lifejacket. On his head was a pure wool stocking cap his mom had knitted.

Gramps was emphatic about wearing wool in the outdoors. He stressed that wool was warm when wet, which meant you could be soaked from chilling rain and still be warm. He said that nylon, acrylic and polyester clothes were good too—he emphasized they worked almost as well as wool, then added, "They're the way to go if you can't afford good wool." He said that outdoors people have a saying—**cotton kills!** So, no blue jeans or flannel shirts, cotton socks, or sweatshirts would be allowed on the trip. Justin's clothes must be wool, nylon, acrylic, or polyester, no exceptions! He would need two pair of shoes—knee-high rubber boots for canoeing, and fabric or leather boots for hiking. Justin was wearing the rubber boots when his grandfather was spirited away—

Cotton kills! Cotton clothes can absorb up to 27 times their weight in water, so they take much longer to dry than wool or synthetics. The moisture in the cotton cools your skin as it evaporates and you get chilled. Cotton clothes are dangerous to wear in cool, damp weather.

his hiking shoes were long gone over the falls.

Swiss Army Knife

Just before they left on their canoe trip, Gramps gave Justin a stout **Swiss Army Knife**. It was the real thing, not a flimsy copy, as his grandfather hated cheap tools. The knife had a locking blade, screwdriver, can-opener, an awl for drilling holes, and a sharp saw. Gramps said the saw was its best feature. He had tied one end of a long nylon cord to the knife and the other end to a belt loop on Justin's pants. "Now, you won't lose your knife if it falls out of your pocket. Lose your knife in the wilderness and you're in big trouble," he said.

Gramps is really smart, thought Justin. An argument here and he might have lost his knife! Besides the knife, Gramps insisted that Justin always have a few things in his pockets including a butane lighter, a compass, an insect head net and repellent, a large cowboy handkerchief, lip balm with sunscreen, a small coil of parachute cord, and an energy bar or some hard candy.

Fly: The best tents have two roofs—an inner, porous roof called a "canopy" and an outer, non-porous roof, called a fly. Inner roofs are breathable, and the outer ones are waterproof, and they're separated by about six inches. Air and perspiration pass easily though the lower canopy, but the waterproof fly above it keeps rain from getting into the tent.

Justin's first order of business was to set up the tarp. Gramps always did that as soon as they camped, that way they'd have a protected place to work and relax. Next, grandpa would pitch the tent and attach the waterproof **fly**. Justin had helped Gramps set up the tarp once, but he didn't remember much. He just did what he was told—mostly held a corner of the tarp or handed Gramps some parachute cord or stakes. Now he wished he'd paid more attention. All he remembered was that Gramps would tie a rope between two trees then tie the tarp to the rope. He wondered why he didn't just tie out the two opposite corners. But he'd been too proud to ask. Now he would have to figure out the tarp by himself.

He located two trees that were about 20 feet apart and tied two opposite corners of the tarp to the trees. Then he staked the back end down. The tarp was flapping wildly in the wind, so he pushed out the center with a long pole he'd cut using the saw on his Swiss Army Knife.

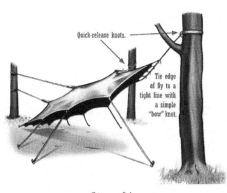

Quick-release knots.

Tie edge of fly to a tight line with a simple "bow" knot.

Storm Lines

The pole reduced the flapping, but it did not eliminate it. Justin remembered that Gramps always tied cords that he called **storm lines** to the sides and front of the tarp, then he staked the cords to the ground and tightened them. Justin copied Gramps and the tarp stopped flapping.

Minutes after the storm lines were in place it began to rain. Not a normal rain, but a real gullywumper! He quickly ducked under the tarp. The trees swayed violently in the wind and water came down in thick sheets. Suddenly, a corner of the fly ripped out and the tarp flattened around him. He just sat there, cross-legged, holding the tarp for dear life and hoping the rain would stop soon. He was miserable, absolutely miserable! He longed for his warm bed at home.

A few minutes later, the rain stopped, and the sun came out. He thought it weird that such a violent storm could pass so quickly. His mood shifted pleasantly when he looked around and saw that everything was fresh and beautiful. He inhaled deeply and marveled that the air smelled clean and wonderful, not like the air back home in smoggy Los Angeles.

Newly energized, he crawled out from under the tarp and went to survey the damage. Except for the torn corner, the tarp was fine. Now he understood why his grandpa always tied the tarp to a rope strung between two trees. He was sure that the corner wouldn't have ripped if he had done that. Next time, he'd do it Grandpa's way. He would fix the corner when he had time with needles and thread from the possibles pack. Luckily, his mom had taught him how to sew buttons and stuff — she said that sewing was a useful skill.

Meanwhile, he would use a trick he saw on a survivor show on TV. He wrapped the torn corner of the tarp around a smooth, golf ball sized rock, then tied a cord around it. Then he pulled the cord drum-tight and tied it to the tree. The **makeshift tarp anchor** worked great! He smiled proudly, thinking, *I am one smart kid!* He pulled out his camera and punched up the photo of Gramps and him by the aerodrone. Gramps was smiling, as if to say, "I'm proud of you, Justin."

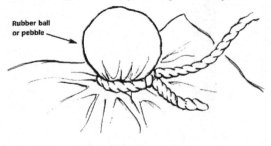

Rubber ball or pebble

Makeshift Tarp Anchor

He suddenly realized that he was ravenously hungry. He'd have to build a fire and cook some food. First the fire, then the food. Making fires was one of the few things he liked about camping, and about which he would willingly take advice from his grandpa. On the last night they had camped together, Justin made the campfire all by himself—and it started with a single flick of his trusty Bic.

His grandpa just looked on silently while he worked. But when the wood burst into bright flames and the flames continued to grow, he walked over, touched Justin's shoulder, and said, "Nice job, son. I know guys who've camped all their lives and can't do fires that well." Then he added, "Fire making is the most important of all the wilderness skills. If you can make a one match fire in the rain, you'll be a hero to your friends!"

Justin thought that line was lame, but right now, he'd give anything to hear Gramps say it. Gramps had told him that he was proud of him many times in the past, but this was one of the few times that Justin thought he deserved the praise. He felt proud that he had done it right.

The rain was short, but it had dumped a lot of water. What earlier had been dead, dry wood was now dead, wet wood. But Justin knew exactly what to do. Gramps had said that rain seldom reached the lower branches of evergreen trees, especially big evergreen trees, and that many of these branches would be dead and dry. Still, some could be damp or wet, and others would be green.

"If they break with a *snap*, they're dead and dry. If they bend but don't break, leave 'em be—they're green," he said. Gramps called these dead, dry branches that broke with a crisp snap, "tinder." He emphasized that tinder must be no thicker than a match. "Thicker wood makes smoke, not fire!" he said.

Once the tinder was aflame it would burn quickly, so he needed thicker wood to hold the flame ready. Gramps called the wood one size more thick "kindling" and said it should range in size from pencil-diameter to as thick as his thumb. *Where to look?* All the wood on the ground was soaking wet, but Gramps had shown him a slick trick.

Gramps had found a dead, downed tree and sawed off a wrist-thick branch and shown Justin the end of the branch he'd cut. Except for a narrow ring of dampness near the bark, the wood was dry. Gramps held the cut end to his nose and smelled it. Justin smelled it too. The wood felt dry against his lips and it had no odor. "This means the wood is dry," said Gramps. Justin had laughed when Gramps showed him the "lips and smell test." But Gramps explained that wet and rotten wood has a strong odor while dry wood has almost none. He added that there were exceptions. Cedar—which smelled wonderful—was one of them.

Many years ago, a forest fire had burned through the area, so dead trees were all around. Justin sawed off a branch from one of them and smelled the cut end. It felt dry to his lips and it passed the smell test, so he dragged it back to camp and sawed it into foot-long pieces. The dry heartwood in the center would make good kindling—but he'd have to split the wood to get it. For this, he'd need the hatchet.

Safe way to split thick logs

"Keeper stick" holds kindling upright

Safe way to split small kindling

Safely Splitting Wood

Justin had helped Gramps before, so he knew the procedure for **safely splitting wood**. He set one of the pieces he'd cut upright on a thick piece of wood. Gramps never split logs on dirt or rock—he always used a wooden splitting block. "It's a lot of work to sharpen an axe—and I like mine razor sharp!" he said. "You're dead meat if you hit the ground with my hatchet!"

Justin set the blade of the axe lightly on the end of the short log and held it firmly with his off-hand, and with his strong hand used a heavy chunk of wood to pound the axe on through, as if the log was a mallet. The piece split with a loud snap—proof that it was bone dry! He continued in this manner until he had a small pile of kindling that was a little thicker than his thumb, then sheathed the little axe and set it near the pile of split kindling.

There was no need to split more wood than was needed to get a bed of coals going. Once they were, whole pieces would burn just fine. He took a break, pleased with all the wood he had cut. While he was sitting there, he noticed a small blister forming where he'd held the axe. *A battle wound,* he thought. Gramps never got blisters—someday he'd be like Gramps.

He decided to build his fire barely under the tarp, figuring the tarp would protect it if it rained again. Gramps told him that the Boy Scouts have a saying, "First, clear the ground three feet around, then build your fire there." Justin willingly accepted this advice—after all, he didn't want to burn up in a forest fire!

He began by constructing a tiny tipi with thin sticks of kindling. Next, he broke some tinder sticks from a dry branch and wadded them into a fist-sized ball. He set the ball inside the tipi. Then he licked his forefinger and raised it high to check the wind's direction. A light breeze was blowing towards him, so he scooted around the tipi so he could light it from the other, upwind side. This way, the breeze would blow the flame into the tinder, not away from it. If, after he lit his fire, he discovered the wind was too strong, he'd just block it with his body.

He spun the spark wheel on his lighter and applied the flame to the tinder. Almost instantly, he had fire! He added more tinder sticks, carefully inserting them directly into the growing flame. When the blaze was burning well, he added split kindling. As the flames grew higher, he added bigger, unsplit wood. He removed his lifejacket and parka—now he was too warm!

For a while, he just sat there and basked in the heat of the flames. He was proud of his "one-Bic-flick" fire. He recalled one of his grandpa's rants, "Most people can't make fires because they add too much wood too fast—and they place the pieces too close together, which smothers the flame. Fires need air—lots of it! You're doing it right if you can see space and light between every piece of wood you burn." Justin stared into the leaping flames. He had done it right. Really right!

Clouds were building. *Seriously, more rain? Better make some food and figure out a bed for the night.* He took one of the freeze-dried meals out of the pack. It was chicken with rice and vegetables. The directions read, "Add 4 cups of boiling water to the aluminized zip-lock pouch and stir thoroughly. Close the bag and let the contents sit for 10 to 12 minutes. Stir and serve."

Suddenly, he stopped reading and bolted upright. Everything he was doing was based on the belief that his grandpa would return shortly. *What if Gramps never comes back?* A chill ran down his back. He had heard that starving was a terrible way to die. And he didn't want to die! But that was exactly what would happen if he ran out of food before he could be rescued. Right then, he decided to make his food last as long as possible—he would eat just enough to keep the hunger pangs away, and no more.

The chicken-rice meal served four, so he would make one-fourth of it and save the rest for later. He filled the Sierra Cup with water and put it on the coals to boil. Then, he poured about three-fourths of the dried food into a piece of aluminum foil and sealed the foil around it. He placed the foil package into the possibles pack. When the water boiled, he poured it into the zipper-lock bag and stirred the food with a stick. Then he sealed the bag and waited. When he thought enough time had passed, he opened the bag and tasted the food.

Yuk! It was awful. Either it hadn't set long enough, or it was just plain bad. He was hungry though and wolfed it down in seconds. Quizzically, he looked at the *serves four* writing on the bag. *Yeah, right!* he thought, *four full mice!* He remembered the leftover cheese, salami, and nuts from lunch and devoured them all.

When he had finished his meal, he thoughtlessly tossed the food bag into the fire.

Yuk! Best way to prepare a "Cook-in-the-bag" freeze-dried meal is to add boiling water to the bag, then set the bag into a pot of near boiling water. Cover the pot and allow the food to sit for several minutes longer than the recommended time. The advertised serving amounts should always be doubled.

Fortunately, he pulled it out before it burned. *How stupid,* he thought, *how could I be so damn dumb?* Suddenly, what had earlier been a useless food bag was now a treasured pot for cooking and hauling water. He walked to the river and washed it out. Then he returned to the fire and the tarp.

Now to rig some sort of bed inside the tarp. But when he went to make the bed, he discovered that the tarp was filled with smoke. It was dead calm, yet smoke was blowing into the tarp. **How could this be?** Well, that was something he'd ask Gramps when he returned. *God, I hope it's soon!* For now, he'd move the fire out from under the tarp—that was what Gramps would do.

He cleared a spot just outside the tarp then moved his fire there. He piled rocks about two feet high behind the fire, hoping the smoke would go towards it. *Success!* The best part was that the rocks reflected heat into the tarp! All he had to do was keep the fire going all night and he'd be warm. Of course, this meant he'd have to gather more wood, but there was plenty of it around.

The nights so far had been cold—in the low forties—but his down sleeping bag was super warm. Unfortunately, it and everything else were long gone. Now, all he had for a bed was a silver space blanket, a plastic tablecloth, and two lifejackets. If Gramps were here, Justin would be complaining, but now that he was all alone, he'd best just get at it.

How could this be? Anything that's close to a fire, like a tarp, your body or a rock, will create a low-pressure area. The hot smoke has higher pressure, so it is drawn towards the low-pressure spots. That's why campfire smoke always follows you! Experienced outdoors people call this low-pressure zone a "smoke eddy."

He set the space blanket on the ground, silver side up, just inside the tarp, with the long side near the fire so his full body would get the reflected heat. Then he placed the tablecloth on top of the space blanket and the two unzipped lifejackets on top of that. He set the hatchet nearby, where he could grab it quickly in the event an animal tried to get his food. Next, he dragged an armful of wood into the shelter. When everything was arranged to his liking, he slipped between the tablecloth and space blanket. For a while, he just watched the brightly burning fire and thought about what tomorrow would bring. But he would worry about that tomorrow. Right now, he was just glad he had food in his belly, a warm fire, and a roof over his head.

He had barely got to sleep when he was awakened by the cold. Strangely, he was warm on top but cold on the bottom. He wondered why he was never cold when he slept inside the tent. Then he remembered his grandpa saying that the ground was bitter cold up north, which was why they had foam-filled pads underneath their sleeping bags. *Well,* he thought, *the lifejackets are filled with foam, maybe they'll make a good mattress.* He set them underneath his body, and almost instantly, the chill was gone. But the fire had burned down and now he was cold on top. *What to do?*

There wasn't much he could think of, other than to keep feeding the fire. He looked at his dwindling supply of firewood, sure it wouldn't last the night. He had almost resigned himself to being cold when he remembered a story he'd read in school, about an early mountain man named Hugh Glass, who was mauled by a grizzly bear in South Dakota in the 1800s.

Glass was badly hurt and left for dead by his friends. They took his prized rifle, tomahawk, and all his possessions. He was alone and more than 200 miles from Fort Kiowa, the nearest American settlement. All he had were the clothes on his back and a burning desire to live. He survived the cold autumn nights by burrowing into the brush and covering himself with leaves and vegetation. Six weeks later, Hugh Glass reached Fort Kiowa, very much alive.

*Cutting live, green **boughs** damages the tree and provides an entryway for insects and disease-causing micro-organisms. Modern campers sleep on insulated foam pads—they are much more comfortable than boughs! "Bough beds" are for emergencies only!*

Justin figured that what worked for Glass should work for him. A clump of spruce trees was nearby. He broke some green **boughs** and brought them back to camp. Then, he rearranged his sleeping system, layering a thick bed of evergreen boughs on the ground followed by the space blanket, silver-side-up. On top of that he placed the unzipped lifejackets for warmth and comfort., then the tablecloth, and another layer of boughs.

When he crawled between the space-blanket and tablecloth layers, both sides of him were warm at last. He grabbed Gramps' book, but decided he was too worn out to read, so he carefully stuffed it back into the possibles pack. It could wait until tomorrow, but somehow, his journal couldn't. He wrote:

June 26, Day 1 alone,

I don't know why I'm writing when I'm so freaked out and there's so much to do. But somehow, I know Gramps would want me to write. It's really scary being out here alone. I wish Gramps were here! I hope he comes back real soon. If he doesn't, I'll have to figure out what to do. Right now, I have enough food for about three days, that's all. It gets cold here at night. But I'm not cold. I made a warm bed from evergreen boughs. I can make it warmer by adding more boughs.

Justin fell asleep.

Sometime during the night, it rained, putting his fire out, but he was warm, dry, and deep in dreamland, not hearing or feeling a drop.

CHAPTER 5 — OTTER LAKE

Henry Jansen bolted upright at the sound of deafening thunder. Lightning flashes lit up the sky in rapid succession as far as he could see. There was smoke on the ridge above him—a large part of the esker was burning! Henry was too tired to care, though. He had survived the long swim to shore, built a fire, and dried his clothes, then burrowed into the brush beneath a towering spruce tree. He just sat there, listening to the thunder and re-counting the day's events.

At first, he had been happy that the men had come to take the drone away. But he also noted that they had been quite unfriendly. Instead of immediately introducing themselves—which was the Northwoods custom—they just stood by the floatplane and talked quietly among themselves. After they had loaded the drone, one of the men smiled and beckoned Henry to come aboard. He said they had a cooler filled with steaks and that Henry could help himself. "It's our way to thank you guys for baby-sitting our little saucer," he explained.

*The **DeHavilland DHC-2 Beaver** is Canada's most famous bush plane. Only 1657 planes were manufactured between 1947 and 1967 but many are still flying today. The Beaver can be fitted with wheels, skis, or floats. Alaskan pilots install balloon-like "tundra tires" so they can land on gravel bars along rivers.*

However, as soon as Henry stepped aboard, he was greeted by a man with a gun. The man pointed the gun at him and said quietly, "Okay, asshole, call the kid in here."

Instead of calling Justin, Henry shouted, "Justin, run!"

The man jerked Henry into a seat and put the gun to his head and told him to "shut the hell up." A minute later, the yellow **DeHavilland Beaver** was airborne. The man,

DeHavilland DHC-2 Beaver

whose name he later learned was Max, blindfolded him and put a pair of earphones on his head.

"Big mistake, the kid's gonna die slow. Storm coming tonight, freezing temperatures. The kid will be dead by morning. Better for him if he'd have just come with us," taunted Max. When Henry asked him what this was all about, Max said he didn't need to know and that he'd be dead in less than an hour.

Henry was remarkably calm when he learned his fate. Maybe it was because he was 75 years old and had lived a good life. Perhaps his time had come, or maybe he was confident there was still a way out. It was Justin that he was more worried about. Justin was just a kid—his whole life was still in front of him.

"Why?" he asked, "Why my grandson?"

"Business, just business. Nothing personal," Max replied coldly. Henry silently glared at the man.

Henry learned that they had planned to push him and Justin over the falls to make their deaths look accidental. They had already taken care of the canoe, and he and Justin would have been next. But when Justin ran away, they decided to leave him to the wolves. A big storm with near-freezing temperatures was coming, so they were sure he would be dead by morning. Everyone would think he had survived the drop over the falls and crawled ashore, only to die that night from **hypothermia**.

Henry would die a different death. They would fly to Otter Lake, about 30 miles away, and drop him into the middle of it. Otter Lake was huge and very cold—around 45 degrees Fahrenheit this time of year— he wouldn't last long in the freezing water. Searchers would think he had died when their canoe went over the falls and that his body had washed down the river to the lake.

Hypothermia means "low temperature" and describes a dangerous drop in body temperature. It occurs when your body is exposed to cold—especially wet-cold—for a long time. It is important to note that most deaths from hypothermia occur in temperatures above freezing.

*An **eddy** is a circular water current that flows in the opposite direction of the main current. If you've ever thrown a stick into a river and watched it float back upstream, you've seen an eddy. Eddies are found near the shoreline and just below exposed rocks in rivers. Fish love eddies because the eddies trap their food. That's something to remember when you go fishing!*

*Another term for "lifejacket" is **PFD**, which stands for "Personal Flotation Device."*

Henry knew that 30 miles was a long way for a body to float, but it was not impossible. Some years ago, a friend lost an expensive paddle when he capsized on the Clearwater River in Alberta, Canada. Two days later, he found it floating in an **eddy**, 40 miles downstream! Bad stuff sometimes happened on remote canoe trips. No one would question how they died.

But Henry wasn't the kind of man who gave up easily. When he learned their plans, he feigned being cold and put up the hood of his parka. Then he secretly pulled the wrist, neck, and waist cords in the jacket as tight as they would go. Water would get in, of course, but slowly.

His thick wool jacket-shirt and wool long underwear would keep him warm, too, at least for a little while. He had always preached that wool was magic. Now, he would be the ultimate test. He wished for his **PFD** but took comfort in the knowledge that if he died, his paddling friends would suspect foul-play because they knew he always wore it. He had known several canoeists who died because they weren't wearing lifejackets, some of them experts!

Henry was afraid he'd drown without a flotation device and was encouraged when he remembered an old Boy Scout trick to make one. As soon as he hit the water, he would quickly remove his nylon river pants and use them to make an inflated buoy. While treading water he would tightly knot the end of each leg, then bring the waist from behind his head into the water in front of him, quickly, trapping air. It would help keep him afloat, and hopefully, above the waves. This was no MacGyver trick—many people had used it to save their lives.

Meanwhile, the plane was bucking through turbulence as they approached the lake. The pilot was freaking out—he said the weather was deteriorating and he didn't want to linger. Max told him to, "Just land the damn thing and we'll push him out fast."

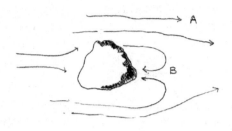

Current Flows Upstream at B, an Eddy

As they were making their approach, Henry heard the pilot say, "Damn! The north end is iced in but there are some open leads to the south, near shore." Max said it didn't matter where they dumped him— the cold water would kill him quick. The moment the pontoons touched water, Max pulled off Henry's earphones and blindfold, opened the cargo door, and pushed him into the icy water.

Henry hit the water hard and half-somersaulted in the waves. He felt water seeping in, but a rush of adrenaline tamed the cold. He quickly removed his pants and did the Boy Scout trick. Seconds later, he was riding high in the waves and kicking hard towards shore. He judged he needed to make it about a quarter mile.

The wind was getting stronger, pushing him along at what seemed a fantastic speed. A sandy beach and a long esker came into view. It would be close, but if he could just hang on a bit longer, he would make it. Given the strong tail wind, he was surprised that the waves were so small, then he remembered that Otter Lake was very shallow, and it had a lot of islands that blocked the wind.

As he neared shore, he heard the drone of the Beaver overhead and looked up. *The bastards are buzzing me!* he thought as the plane swooped close to him then quickly rose again to clear the trees. Just then, a thick, black cloud came out of nowhere. It was followed by a howling wind— a **microburst**—that caused the plane to stall and lose control. It hung precariously as it lost speed, then crashed behind the esker. The powerful wind lasted only about a minute, but that was long enough to crash the plane. As suddenly as it began, the microburst was gone, replaced by a gentle breeze, and the sun came out.

*A **microburst** is a small but powerful wind that pushes down, rather than up, like a tornado. They are extremely hazardous to aircraft and are found in strong thunderstorms.*

Henry was ecstatic! *Couldn't have happened to nicer guys,* he thought. *If I'm still alive tomorrow, I'll hike over to that wreck and see what I can find.* Minutes later, Henry washed ashore—he'd been in the water for nearly ten minutes, he thought. He was very cold—but he was alive! Now, more than ever, he truly believed in the magic of wool.

Henry's lips were blue, and he was shivering violently. He needed a fire, now! There were some paper birch trees at the top of the esker that he could see, and he headed for them as fast as he could go. He peeled a layer of bark off one of the trees and shredded the bark into a ball, then got out his lighter and spun the spark wheel. Nothing. He spun it again; still nothing. Then he remembered that he had forgotten to "blow dry" the wheel and jet—important if the lighter is wet. So, he put the lighter near his lips and blew on it half-a-dozen times. When he tried again, the lighter worked! He lit the **birch bark** and it burst into flame. *Sweet mercy!*

There were lots of dead, dry sticks scattered on the ground, and he gathered a handful and poked them into the developing flames. The flames grew higher, the fire grew warmer. He stopped shivering and his lips turned red again. He stripped off his wet clothes and set them on sticks he'd propped by the fire. Then, for a long time, he just sat and basked in the warmth of the blaze and worried about Justin. He smiled slightly, thinking, *at the very least, the kid can make a one-match fire!* After all, he was a Jansen.

*Except in an emergency, please don't strip **birch bark** from trees. Stripping bark is illegal, and it can kill the tree. If you must build a fire with birch bark, please take it from a dead, downed tree or from pieces that are lying on the ground.*

After about an hour his clothes were dry, so he put them back on. The sky was darkening again, only this time, it was black as far as he could see. He estimated that the rain would come soon, and that it would be heavy, and it would be long. *Better find a dry spot to spend the night soon.*

He kicked sand over the fire then walked to a large spruce tree. He cut an armful of boughs with his sheath knife and arranged them into

31

a bed. Shortly after he crawled between the boughs, it began to rain — lightly at first, then with a determined *tap, tap, tap* — but the limbs above stopped the rain. He remained warm and dry, and lay there thinking, wondering why they hadn't taken his sheath knife and Leatherman multi-tool and everything that was in his pockets. *If they had, searchers would question his "accidental" death,* he realized. Everyone knew that Henry always went prepared!

He dozed off to sleep to the persistent patter of rain. He was warm and dry, and very much alive. Somehow, he knew that Justin was too.

CHAPTER 6 — REALITY

Justin awoke to the buzz of mosquitoes and the warmth of a rising sun. He put on his insect head net and re-started the fire. Then he filled the Sierra cup with water and put it on to boil. Breakfast would be an energy bar with bouillon soup and rice. For a while, he just sat there thinking. He'd been alone for 18 hours now and he was beginning to doubt that his grandfather would return. He knew that Gramps had arranged for a float plane to pick them up at the mouth of the river on July 22, which was 25 days from today. When Justin had questioned what would happen if they weren't there on July 22, Gramps said, "Big problem! Trust me, we'll be there!"

Justin pushed the question. "And what if we're not? What if we're just not?"

Gramps shot back, "Justin, that would happen only if we had an emergency. I don't like emergencies, but I do plan for them, I wouldn't risk us. And that's why we're bringing a satellite phone. But it's only for emergencies. Do you understand?"

Justin had nodded weakly, then he took out his journal and wrote "JULY 22" in big, block letter, then circled it and drew stars around it.

His thoughts turned to the future. *What if Gramps doesn't come back?* Yeah, what if he didn't? If he stayed in this obscure channel, no one would ever find him. He decided that if Gramps didn't return, he would go to where the float plane would be.

It was his only chance to control his fate but going downriver alone would be dangerous and scary—better to figure out the satellite phone and stay right here! Suddenly, his mood changed to anger. "Why can't

I figure out the damn phone?!" he screamed. He thought there must be a code—probably two or three numbers. After he'd calmed down, he removed the phone from its box and turned it on.

While it was starting up, he opened his journal to a blank page and drew a table. He decided to try different combinations of numbers until he hit on the one that worked. He would record the numbers in the table so that he didn't repeat them. He believed that if he went about this methodically—like playing a game—he'd eventually get them right. He just hoped it wouldn't take too long! First, he tried the single numbers 0 through 9, followed by his home area code and the number. No luck. *Dammit!* Next, he started on the two-digit codes. There were a lot of combinations so it would take some time to try them all. After about 10 minutes of trying numbers, he gave up in disgust. Now, more pissed off than ever, he turned off the phone and shoved it back into its waterproof case.

As he slowly ate his breakfast, his thoughts turned again to food. He would finish the partial chicken-rice meal today. That would leave one freeze-dried meal plus about a cup of rice, 20-some bouillon cubes, and two energy bars—enough for maybe three days, at most. *Three days?* He was terrified! *Enough for just three days!* He had to find food, and fast. *But what if I can't, I'll die!* Then he remembered Gramps' 3-3-3 rule, "You can live three minutes without air, three days without water, and three weeks without food." Okay, food could wait, but not for long.

If he only had his slingshot—the one his dad had given him. It was a genuine Wrist Rocket Hunter-Survival model. It had a built-in wrist-stabilizer for extra power. With good ammo—marble-sized steel balls—he could whack a ping-pong ball at 30 feet. That would easily kill a rabbit or squirrel. He hadn't seen any rabbits, but there were lots of little ground squirrels. They were cute and fun to watch, but they were also food, and they would be an easy target for him.

He remembered when he got the slingshot. It was the day after he got kicked out of school for fighting. There was this little kid, Ralphie, in his English class who had cerebral palsy. Ralphie talked different, and his arms and legs kind of flopped around when he walked, but he was really nice, and smart too—he was on the B+ honor roll. Most everyone, except Rick, was kind to him. Rick would imitate his walk and how he talked. When he passed Ralphie in the hall, he'd dump his books and laugh.

It was on a Monday when the fight happened. Everyone was passing in the halls. Rick passed Ralphie and dumped his books again, then he laughed and made gestures with his hands. For some reason that day it just crossed a line and enough was enough. Justin was smaller than Rick, but he was so mad that he didn't care. He got into Rick's face and yelled, "Hey, asshole, why don't you pick on someone your own size?" At this, Rick threw a punch, and Justin ducked and threw one of his own. It landed smack on Rick's nose, and instantly, there was blood all over the place. Seconds later, two teachers tore them apart and brought them to the principal's office. They were both suspended for three days.

When Justin went to his locker to get his stuff before leaving early that day, his English teacher walked over and put her hand on his shoulder and said, "Justin, you were great today and I'm very proud of you. Rick deserved what he got, you didn't!"

As he was leaving some kids standing by the door gave him air-five's as he walked out, but best of all, that night, Sara called to say that she liked what he did. Her phone call alone was worth getting suspended. It happened nearly a year ago, but Justin still felt wronged for getting suspended. His mom and dad agreed. Instead of punishing him for fighting, his dad took him shopping the next day and bought him the slingshot.

Justin lived with his mom. He only saw his dad a few times a month. His parents were separated, and their divorce was nearly done. He loved his dad and his dad loved him. But his dad was always screwing up. Justin had heard someone call him a functioning-alcoholic, meaning that though he had a substance abuse problem, he could still function as a member of society. He was a brilliant software engineer—a killer app he developed made millions for the company he worked for. They knew he often drank at work, but because he was so good, they looked the other way.

Worse, he'd start more heavily drinking as soon as he got home, and by supper, he was roaring drunk. He was never mean or hurtful when he was bombed, and everyone liked him—he even knew his mom still loved him, she just couldn't take the pain of watching it happen anymore. While Justin wished it weren't so, it was part of the reality he was used to. Now he needed to return to the present. *Enough!*

he thought. *I gotta focus on what is, not what was or what should be. First thing is to gather more firewood and improve my bed, then I'll see about food.*

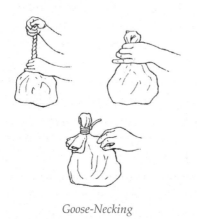

Goose-Necking

As soon as he finished his soup, he returned the Sierra cup to the possibles pack—it had become a treasured possession and he didn't want to lose it. As he was closing the pack, his eyes focused on the loop of bungee cord that was sewn to the mouth of the waterproof liner bag inside it. Gramps lined every pack with a waterproof bag so its contents would stay dry in rain or a capsize and used a special procedure called **goose-necking** to seal the bag. First, he'd tightly twist the neck then fold it over. Then he'd use the bungee loop like a rubber band to hold it in place. He claimed that the twist and fold prevented leaks—and unlike ties, the elastic band wouldn't loosen up. Gramps had told Justin stories about people who didn't use waterproof bags. Everything got soaking wet because they were less cautious, and he emphasized that it takes days to dry a sleeping bag in the sun or by a campfire. "Meanwhile, you won't be having a good time!" he said.

He wondered if he could use the bungee cord to make a slingshot, so he untied the knot at the end and stretched out the loop. It was about a foot-and-a-half long—long enough. He tested the stretch. It was stiffer than the rubber on his Wrist-Rocket, but not so stiff that he couldn't pull it. *Forget the firewood and food—I'm gonna make a slingshot!*

He found a paper birch tree and sawed off a thick Y-shaped limb. He whittled it to fit his hand. It was somewhat thicker than the frame of his metal one, but the bungee cord was stiffer too, so he figured he needed thicker wood. The bungee was too short to knot around the arms of the slingshot, so he sawed a notch in the top of each Y. Then, he knotted the ends of the bungee and inserted them into the notches in the Y's.

He pulled back hard on the bungee to cinch the knot tight. Then he pulled again, this time as hard as he could. *Yes! I'm in business!* He was still a little concerned that the bungee might come out of the notch and whack him in the face when he shot, so he decided to anchor it in place with wire from the repair kit. Next, he cut a piece of canvas out of the flap of the possibles pack. He folded the canvas over the bungee cord and duct taped the sides together. This would be the ammo pocket. He would have to turn his hand sideways to hold the ammo in the pocket, but that would be no problem.

He gathered some round pebbles and tried his new tool. A white, baseball-sized rock about 25 feet away was his target. He let a pebble fly. It landed just beyond the rock. He tried again, still too far. The third time he shot, it hit the rock, dead on. The bungee was stiffer than the elastic on his Wrist Rocket, and of course, there was no wrist support, which made full-draws much harder, but there was enough power to kill a squirrel or bird or rabbit—if he could hit one. He would practice until he could! His depression broke. Suddenly, he was on cloud nine. He believed—really believed—that he would survive.

He spent the rest of the day gathering wood, improving his bed, and practicing his aim. By supper time, he could hit the rock every time. He thought that if Gramps could see him now, he'd be really proud.

He finished the chicken-rice meal for supper, then for a while, just sat there thinking. He decided that tomorrow he would arise early and spend the day foraging for food. The river was filled with tasty fish—if only he had a pole to catch them. Then, he remembered the book. Maybe it would give him some ideas. He opened to the title page. There was an inscription that read:

"To my wonderful grandson, Justin. I hope you grow to love wild places as much as me—and have the courage to protect them from development. I'll always remember our canoe trip together. It was special, just like you.
Love, Grandpa Henry."

The words brought moisture to his eyes. Irritated with himself, he rubbed them away. "I'm sorry, Gramps, I'm sorry. Please come back, please! I promise I'll be good if you come back. I promise, I promise." Then, with new determination, he turned his attention to the book. A chapter entitled "Survival" caught his eyes. He turned to it and found a paragraph called "How to Catch Fish Without a Proper Hook and Line." The opening sentence read, "You can't make something out of nothing—which is why you should always carry these essentials with you when you leave the beaten path."

The list included everything that Justin had on his body or in the possibles pack. For the first time in his life, Justin was totally absorbed by what he was reading in a book. Here, alone, he took comfort in Gramps' words. He took out his camera and looked again at the photo of him and Gramps by the aerodrone. "Thanks, Gramps," he said softly.

Then, he piled the fire high, put away the book, and grabbed his journal.

June 27, Day 2 alone,

It's hard being here all alone. I decided that if Gramps doesn't come back tomorrow, I'm going to go to the float plane. It's a long way. 200 miles! It will be scary, but I have to do it. If I don't, I'll die here!!! One day, Gramps and I canoed 28 miles and it wasn't hard. I think walking is easier than canoeing. Faster too. A lot faster if it's windy! Heck, I ran track and can run 20 miles in a day.

CHAPTER 7 — THE AIRPLANE

Henry was up with the morning sun. There was work to do, and securing food and shelter were at the top of his list. He emptied his pockets and surveyed the contents. Besides his sheath knife and Leatherman multi-tool, he had two butane lighters, an orienteering compass, 12 feet of parachute cord, a thick rubber band, lip balm with sunscreen, a Leatherman micro-tool, a large cotton handkerchief, an insect head-net and repellent, an energy bar, and a few pieces of hard candy.

He smiled when he saw these things because he knew that, with them, he could survive. He casually re-started the fire, then ate the energy bar and candy. For a long time, he sat there thinking, staring at the fire-blackened trees on the horizon. The fire that had burned so brightly last night was out. Not a hint of smoke remained. He had watched the plane go down behind the esker—a mile or two away. If he could find it, there might be some stuff that he could use. Anyway, it was worth checking. He took a compass bearing of where he thought the wreck might be, then he extinguished the fire and started walking. The blaze had burned the far side of the ridge and the valley below it in a haphazard pattern. *Lucky last night's rain put the fire out—otherwise, I might be toast.*

Ninety minutes passed and there was still no sign of the plane. He was ready to quit walking when he saw a strange-looking black tree. Could it be the burned tail of an airplane? When he got closer, he confirmed that it was. The plane had crashed in a pond, just below the ridge. It was nose down in the water—everything forward of the cargo doors was under water. From a distance, its blackened tail looked just like a burned tree. Henry didn't think a search plane would see it from the air.

He studied the plane for several minutes before deciding what to do. It was barely 50 feet from shore, so he could easily swim out to it. He removed his clothes and boots—he didn't want to get them wet again. Then he buckled on his belt, which contained his sheath knife and multi-tool. When he reached the plane, he discovered that one of the cargo doors was open. He peered inside and saw two bodies in the front seats—they were submerged in water and pinned tightly against the firewall. Their eyes were open wide, and their hair swayed eerily, like weeds in the wind.

It was a grotesque sight, but Henry was pleased that they were dead. He looked around curiously. *Where is number three?* A chill ran down his spine. One man was missing—could he have gotten out alive? If so, Henry was in deep trouble! It was too dark inside the plane to see very much, so he just felt around with his hands, hoping that he might find something useful. He gave up quickly, thinking that whatever was in back that wasn't bolted down likely either floated out or burned, and so cautiously climbed out and onto a pontoon.

Just as he was stepping into the water, something on the side of the pontoon caught his eye. *An axe—a full-sized axe!* Glory be, what a find! He unstrapped the axe from its riveted aluminum sheath and took it. As he was doing this, another thought emerged. Why not also take the cargo door? He could make a grill or pot from the aluminum skin. All he had to do was pop the hinge bolts and it would come right off.

Back on shore, he air-dried in the sun. As he dressed, he noticed what appeared to be a body floating in the water. He walked to the water's edge for a closer look. It was Max! "Yes! The bastards are all dead!" he yelled loudly.

Henry swam out and retrieved the body—the man's clothing and shoes would be useful. He brightened considerably when he removed the man's jacket and discovered a Glock 19, semi-automatic, 9 mm pistol in a leather shoulder holster. The Glock was different than the Colt 1911 that he carried when he was an officer in the army in the 1960s, but he was sure he could figure it out.

He removed the magazine and popped out the bullets. There were 15, plus one in the chamber. He wiped them with his handkerchief and set them in the sun to dry. Military ammo was waterproofed, civilian ammo wasn't—he hoped the gun would fire, but he wasn't sure. He searched the body and found another full magazine. In all, he had 31 bullets—enough to last several weeks. He used a smooth, straight stick and a patch cut from his cowboy hanky to dry the inside of the barrel. Then he daubed some chap stick on another patch and pushed it down the barrel. He reminded himself aloud, "A rusted gun can't be trusted!"

Henry believed that those who sent the plane would come looking for it. And he figured they had probably tracked it to this very spot. So, he had to dispose of Max's body. He thought that if they found it and discovered that his clothes and gun were missing, they would come looking for him. He dragged the corpse into the bush and covered it with burned debris. As he was working, he spied some water lilies growing near the edge of the pond.

Food! he thought excitedly. He collected a bunch of the floating plants and tied them to the airplane door. Then he used the door like a sled and hauled everything back to camp.

Henry was finishing supper when he saw a ground squirrel. It was standing on its hind legs about 20 feet away. He thought it would be nice to have some meat with his vegetables, and while he hated to waste a bullet on such a small animal, he needed to know if the gun worked. If it did, he could bag a muskrat or a rabbit, or maybe a big fat goose. Silently, he sat down, and while holding the pistol firmly with both hands, braced his forearms on his knees. He took a deep breath and let half of it out. He aimed just below the neck, so that if the shot went slightly high or low, he'd still have squirrel for supper.

He *slowly* squeezed the trigger. There was a loud *bang* and the squirrel was his. Surprisingly, he had hit it in the head, a very difficult shot even at this short range. He cleaned the squirrel and placed it on a spit over the fire. There wasn't much meat there, maybe three bites, but with the water lily tubers, it would make a meal.

While it was roasting, he used the axe to cut a large square of aluminum out of the cargo door. He found a round basket-ball-sized rock and set the aluminum piece on top of it. Then, using the rock as mold, he pounded the metal to the shape of a bowl. When it was done, he thought proudly, *Got me a pot.* He filled the pot with water and put it on the fire. Then, he cut up the water lily tubers and placed them into the water. Things were looking better—just had to keep things up. After eating, he would spend the remaining daylight working on his shelter. Tomorrow, he'd make a fish trap. Then, he'd formulate a plan to find Justin.

Meanwhile, back at the International Finance Institute in Chicago, Frank screamed at Geek.

"What do you mean the plane went down and the drone's toast? That's $30 million, Geek! $30 million down the drain!" Suddenly, Frank's face went white. "We're gonna have Feds on our ass fast if they find that drone and link it to us. I ain't goin' back to prison over *your* screw-up! You better fix it, Geek, and fast!"

Eyes wide, Geek stuttered, "Got it covered, Boss, been on it since morning! I know exactly where it went down, and I got a chopper and three of our best guys on the way. Don't worry—they didn't file a flight plan, so the cops won't know that the plane went down, let alone where it went down. I told 'em to recover the drone then torch the plane and get the hell outta there. Don't worry, boss, there's lotsa crashed planes in the north. They won't think twice if they find this one."

"You better be right, Geek, or you'll be toast just like that drone!"

CHAPTER 8 — THE FALLS

Justin was up with the sun, excited to go fishing and anxious to fill his belly. He decided that if Gramps didn't return today, he would stock up on fish then head down-river tomorrow. He and Gramps had caught a few **northern pike** earlier in the trip, and right now, he could taste them all. Oh, how he wished that a nice fat fish, any fish, would suddenly appear for breakfast. Instead, there were two bouillon cubes and the last of the rice, about half-a-cup. Supper would be the last freeze-dried dinner or hopefully, fresh fish.

Northern Pike

He turned to the page in the book that described how to catch a fish without a hook. It read:

"Most of the fish in northern Canada and Alaska are very hungry and will bite on anything. You don't need fancy bait, anything that moves or glitters will work. When I was a boy scout at summer camp, an expert fishing guide came to our camp one evening and entertained us with a story. He said that fish were so easy to catch here that flashy commercial lures weren't necessary. Laughing, he described how he'd bet his client five bucks that he could catch a fish without a hook. His method was to tear a strip of cloth from his bright-colored bandana and tie it directly to the fishing line. Then he'd cast out his

"lure," *jiggling it as he slowly reeled it in. 'A northern pike's teeth slant inward,' he explained. 'They catch on the cloth and I get 'em every time!' Then, he warned us not to wear any shiny rings on our fingers when we were fishing. He said that if you jiggle your ring finger in water, a northern pike will bite it for sure."*

The book then described how to make fishing line by "twining," or twisting narrow strips of fibrous plants to form cord, a technique developed by the American Indians, and how to make fishing line from parachute cord by stripping out the many thin cords inside. The latter was easier method, and since Justin had para cord, he had all the fishing line he needed in less than five minutes. The lines were a bit thicker than commercial fishing line, but they were at least white, so hopefully, they wouldn't scare the fish.

Lastly, he found a tip that a barbless fishhook could be made by bending a safety pin to shape. *Okay—line, handkerchief, and safety pins— I've got everything I need except a pole.* He cut one from a nearby tree and tied the line to it. Then he sliced a strip from his bandana and tied it to the line. The excitement mounted and he could already taste fresh fish! Gramps had said that the fishing is usually **good below a falls,** so that was where he would go. It was a half mile hike to the river below, but it would be worth it if he could get just one fish. He figured he'd spend most of the day away from camp, so he brought the possibles pack with him. He didn't want any animals getting into what little food he had.

Once below the falls, he picked a promising eddy and dropped his line into the water. Then he started to jig. He had barely begun, when *wham!* Something hit his lure. Instinctively, he jerked the pole skyward. *Nothing!* The fish was gone. "Guess that wasn't a northern," he muttered to himself. He decided to add a hook, unwilling to be the guinea pig testing the limits of the hungry-fish legend. He used the notch on the can-opener of his Swiss army knife to bend a diaper pin into the shape of a hook. There was no barb, of course, but Gramps had said that was a handicap only if you didn't know what you were doing. He emphasized that barbed hooks often injured fish that you didn't want to keep. Then he added that the fishing up here was so good that it didn't matter if you lost a few.

Justin tied the hook to the strip of cloth and went back to jigging. A few minutes later, it was wham! again. Only this time, Justin was ready. As soon as he felt the tug, he snapped the pole upward, and glory be—a huge northern pike flew off the lure and landed in the bush behind him. He ran to it and quickly killed it with a rock. It was huge—about two feet long—the biggest fish he'd ever caught and enough for several meals! A flood of warmth washed over him when he realized that he

Fishing is Usually Good Below a Falls

wouldn't starve after he'd finished the food in the possibles pack. He thought, *If I can catch one fish, I can catch more! And if I can catch more, I can make it to the airplane!* But his stomach was growling, so he decided to return to camp and cook this one now. Before he left, he snapped tons of pictures of the fish with the hankie strip in its mouth, just so later, everyone would believe him!

As he was walking up the trail, he heard the whir of a helicopter. He looked up—it was following the river, heading north. He hollered and waved his arms, did jumping jacks. *Come on, please see me!* Nothing. The chopper just kept on going. Suddenly, the thrill of catching the fish was replaced by depression. He cursed himself for not having a proper signal ready—a smoky fire that was ready to light, the silver space blanket staked out in the sun, an SOS built from rocks or logs, anything. *The mirror!* He remembered that the mirror on his compass would have been accessible. *Damn! How could I have forgotten that!* He had missed a chance at rescue and vowed to do better next time.

When the helicopter reached the south end of Otter Lake, it turned inland to the pond where the Beaver had gone down. When it found the wreck, it landed and spent quite a bit of time on the ground. Henry came running at the sound of the chopper—he thought he was being rescued! But he stopped cold when he saw it turn toward the Beaver.

How did they know the Beaver had crashed? And where? He was sure the locator beacon in the tail of the airplane had not been activated, it had probably burned up in the fire! But these guys knew exactly where the Beaver crashed, and that worried him. When the helicopter lifted off again, it flew slowly over his camp and paused briefly, then turned south and flew away. Henry was relieved they hadn't seen him. If they had, it could have been war. There was no coming back from those guys! He patted the Glock and thought, *Glad I got you, babe!*

Boiled fish are delicious! Cut fillets into one-inch chunks and place in boiling water or soup. Cook about five minutes; do not over-cook.

Tripod fish is a cooking method in which a cord is run through the mouth and gills of a large gutted but not scaled or skinned fish. It is then hung over a roaring fire, often from a tripod. The skin will blacken, while the meat will cook in about 15 minutes.

Planked fish is best for smaller fish. Clean the fish, cut off the head, and split the body along the backbone—it will open like a book. Then attach the split fish with nails or whittled wooden pegs to a board set next to a roaring fire.

Fish in general is ready when it becomes chalky white and can be flaked with a fork.

Justin had watched Gramps fillet fish, so he knew roughly how to prepare them. *How to cook them, though.* Gramps either fried the fillets in cooking oil or he cut them into chunks and **boiled them**, but Justin had no pots or pans, so he didn't know what to do. He thought the book might provide a clue, so he skimmed the index.

Sure enough, there were several options. The easiest, was **Tripod Fish**, an old-time way to cook large fish without dirtying pots and pans. Another method, used by early trappers, called **Planked Fish**, was said to work best with smaller fish.

This was a big fish, so he lashed a tripod together and set it and the fish over the fire. The fish blackened almost immediately—it looked like it was burning up! But ohhh, it smelled so good. His mouth watered. *How long is 15 minutes?* It felt like ages and he didn't have a watch. To test it, he made a two-pronged **fork from a green stick** and scraped off some meat from time-to time and tasted it. He kept tasting and tasting

and tasting some more. Before the fish was done, he had eaten half of it. It was absolutely incredible, the best fish he'd ever had! *I could live on fish!* he thought, and, *If I can catch just one fish like this every day, I'll make it home alive.* He thought about Gramps. Was he dead or alive? Now, more than ever, he wanted Gramps to be here, to see what he had done.

Tripod Fish, Mmm Good!

When he had satisfied his hunger, he wrapped what was left of the fish in aluminum foil and secured his treasure inside the possibles pack. Then, he sat and watched the fire. Now well-fed and clear-headed, he pondered two issues he had to address before he headed out to meet the airplane.

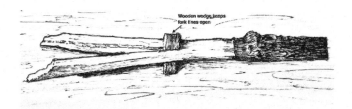

Fork Made From a Green Stick

First, animals would smell any food that he carried on his hike, his fish included, and a slingshot might not be enough to keep them away. What he needed was a spear—one with a sharp stone point. And second, Gramps had clearly marked on the map the best campsites and fishing spots and all the portages that bypassed dangerous rapids. To find them, he would have to learn how to read the map and use his compass. So first, he would make a spear, then he would read—no, study—the "Map & Compass" chapter in the book. He could not afford to get lost!

It took him quite a while to find a branch that was straight enough, long enough, and thick enough to make a strong spear from. He discarded the possibility of using a fire-tempered wooden point. A stone point would be stronger. He searched the shoreline for more than an hour before he found a thin, sharp rock that would work.

He sawed a deep notch in one end of the wooden shaft and epoxy-glued the rock into the notch. While the glue was setting, he tightly wrapped the joint with wire from the repair kit. At last, he had a spear. *A real spear!*

Next, he planned his trip down-river. He studied the map to make sure that he had the best route to where the float plane would land. He estimated he could hike about 15 miles a day—that is, if he could catch enough fish to maintain enough energy. He absolutely had to find good fishing every day, and he realized now that Gramps' great map notes could be lifesavers! He bowed his head slightly in humility and softly said, "Thanks, Gramps."

Then he returned to the map and traced his finger downstream to where he saw a note that read, "Great camp, terrific fishing—got one with nearly every cast!" A penciled arrow pointed to some small brown circles nearby. Justin wondered what the circles meant. He pushed the thought out of mind. Terrific fishing was at mile 93, just 31 miles away—a determined two-day walk. He would go there and stock up on fish for a day or two, then continue on.

He planned to start early tomorrow morning. But how would he know when he'd reached the treasured campsite at mile 93? Was there some identifiable landmark there? He would have to find out what the little circles meant. He cursed himself again for not listening when Gramps tried to show him how to read the map. Now he'd have to figure it out for himself. He couldn't afford to screw up and miss that good campsite, so he decided to read that "Map & Compass" chapter.

Justin's teachers were right when they said he was smart. His problem was that he didn't care enough to focus. Now he did, big time! Indeed, he was so engrossed in the chapter that it would have taken a thunderclap to break his attention. He learned that those little circles were **contour lines**—they connected points of equal elevation above sea level. They were used to indicate the location and height of hills, the depth of valleys and the direction that rivers flowed. Lines that were close together indicated a steep hill, lines that were farther apart indicated more gentle hills. The camp at mile 93 was on a hill, but there were lots of hills of nearly equal height along the river. How would he know which one was the right one? He had no way to

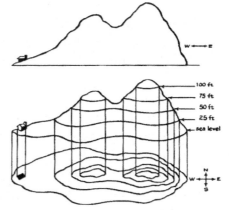

Contour Lines Connect Points of Equal Elevation

measure distance, so how would he know when he'd gone exactly 31 miles?

Then he remembered the GPS. If he could program it to the campsite, his problems would be solved. He wished he had paid attention when Gramps programmed in waypoints. Still, he was sure he could figure it out. He turned on the GPS. When it had accessed enough satellites, a screen with two sets of long numbers appeared. He had no idea what they meant. He pushed the arrow button which took him to the map screen. There was a cursor that showed his location on a very small-scale map. When he pushed the "+" button to enlarge the map, everything became blocky and confusing. The more he zoomed in, the foggier the map became.

He didn't get it, the GPS in his mom's car had a great map, so he must be doing something wrong. There was a chapter on GPS navigation in the book that he'd have to read it, but not right now. It was getting late and he needed rest. Tomorrow would be a long and tiring day. Before he lay down to sleep, he tried the satellite phone again. Still no luck. Disappointed, he built the fire high. Then he set the spear and slingshot beside him.

He was just dozing off to sleep when he heard howls. He bolted upright as a chill ran down his spine. There was no mistaking the howl of wolves, and they were just outside his camp! He grabbed his spear as he rolled out of bed, then tossed wood on the smoldering fire. As the flames picked up, he saw two sets of glowing greenish-orange eyes, 25 yards away. They flickered like candle flames. Justin had never heard wolves before, let alone seen them. When he'd asked Gramps if there were wolves around here, Gramps said, "Oh yeah, lots of 'em here, but don't worry, they hardly ever attack people." Justin hoped that "hardly ever" meant "not now!"

He tossed more wood on the fire and the flames grew higher. Justin continued to stare into their eyes. He was scared, terrified even, and the wolves didn't move and neither did he. He had the spear poised and ready. Then he remembered the slingshot. He launched a marble-sized stone aimed just below the eyes of one of them. There was a high-pitched yelp, and suddenly, they were gone. *Oh my God,* he thought, *I can't believe I just whacked a wolf!*

He piled more wood on the fire, determined to keep it burning all night. He was too keyed up to sleep, so for a long time, he just clung to the spear and stared into the night. Then he had an urge to get out his journal; he began to write.

June 28, Day 3 alone,

Dear Mom and Dad, I was really scared today!!! A big pack of wolves came into camp and tried to eat me! I made a slingshot and wacked a wolf. It ran away. Thanks, Dad, for teaching me how to shoot. If the wolves come back and kill me, know that I tried to fight!!! I think I'm getting stronger. I love you both and I'm sorry I've been such a pain. I'm still trying to figure out the satellite phone, but so far, no luck.

CHAPTER 9 — GONE FISHING

While Justin was making his spear, Henry was fishing, and while he fished, he was thinking. Thinking about how desperately he wanted to get back to Justin. *But how?* He was 30 miles down-river and he was a man without a boat. Hiking back to the falls would be impossible—he would have to skirt several lakes and swamps, which could take weeks, if he could make it at all. *I need a boat.* He thought about building a raft, but the available wood was too small. Besides, a raft would be too slow and heavy to portage around the many rapids and falls. *There's got to be a way!* He had promised Justin's mom that all would be okay, and well, it wasn't. He couldn't go home without Justin.

At a loss, he turned his thoughts to the quiet pool where minnows were congregating. He decided that the best way to catch them was with his insect head net. He bent some green sticks into hoops and tied them to the opening of the net. Then he lashed a short pole to the net so that he could handle it without being seen by the fish. He scooped several netfuls of the little fish into the bowl that he had made from the airplane door. When he had enough, he gutted them, then tossed them back into the bowl. They would make a tasty addition to the water lily tubers. He would decide later whether he would boil them up in his metal bowl or grill them on green sticks over a smoldering fire.

As he was heading back to camp, his thoughts returned to the men in the helicopter. They would have found two bodies, not three, in the burned-out plane. Hopefully, they would think that one man got out and had drowned in the pond or was lost in the bush. Maybe they were just searching for the missing man when they flew slowly over his camp. It wasn't as if he had much there to draw their attention. *If they had suspected something, they would have landed and checked it out,* he reasoned. At that, he put the chopper out of mind and again focused on Justin. Was he dead? He also pushed that thought away. Justin was smart, Henry just hoped he would read the book and learn how to survive. He spontaneously yelled, at the top of his lungs, "You're alive, Justin, I know you're alive! Just read the book. Please read the book!"

CHAPTER 10 — LOST

Justin was up at dawn, eager to start down the river. He finished the fish then took down the tarp and packed the possibles pack. Then he ripped a page from his journal and wrote a note that he was going downriver. He wrapped the note in a piece of birch bark and taped the bark to the branch of a prominent tree. Remembering his promise to take pictures, he posed for a selfie. Then, spear in hand, he set off down the portage trail.

The portage ended in a jumble of boulders at the water's edge. From this point on, Justin had to make his own trail. He found a narrow animal trail that paralleled the river, and he followed it until it petered out. Ahead was a high hill with a sheer cliff that faced the river. He skirted around it, which brought him deeper into the wilderness and away from the river. Soon, he encountered a large patch of trees that had been blown down by wind, and he had to climb over or under each.

Progress was painfully slow. His socks were wet from sweat and there was a blister forming on his heel. He wished he'd had his tennis shoes. He found another animal trail and followed it, which made progress easier, but took him farther and farther from the river.

By noon, he realized he was lost. He panicked and started to run but almost immediately tripped and fell. For a while, he just sat there on the ground, holding his head in his hands and wondering what to do. He had to be strong—and smart. He had to figure out where he was and where the river was. He stared at the map blankly. The river ran almost due north for about 10 miles, then it turned west. He was on the east, or right side of the river from his perspective. *But where?* Well, all he had to do was head west and he would run into the river—eventually. He set his compass for west, to 90 degrees, and loosely followed that direction. He walked for what seemed like hours without the river coming into view. He must be doing something wrong, but what?

He came to a stream. It ran west, towards the river, but he was too hungry and tired to continue on, and there was water here, so he built a fire and cooked the freeze-dried meal. He was so hungry that he ate all of it. He realized this was the last of his food, but he just couldn't help himself. He was too tired to set up the tarp, so he just wrapped himself in it and fell asleep by the fire.

He woke up to the bare light of dawn. The fire had gone out and he was cold. He had a bad feeling. He'd gone barely three miles and already he was lost. *Getting to the airplane is impossible!* Still, he had to do it.

Justin re-started the fire, then washed his face in the stream and took a long drink of water. Then he set off to follow the stream westward, towards the river. He had been walking for only a few minutes, when he suddenly stepped into bright sunlight. Before him was the river! He was so surprised that he let out a holler. He had been lost and now he was found! Well, sort of.

He still had no idea exactly where he was, but the east channel he had been following was narrow and shallow. Here, the river was wide and deep, so he was sure he had passed where the two channels joined back up. He wondered how he would ever find the camp at mile 93. And, he was hungry again, so he rigged a pole and jigged for fish. He jigged and jigged. Nothing. Well, he would just have to ignore his hunger and keep going. The country was opening-up a bit, so walking became easier. Still, much of the time, he couldn't see the river.

By late afternoon, he was delirious from hunger. He had run out of energy and needed to find something to eat. His path was blocked, too. Ahead was a marshy inlet that he would have to walk around. *That might take hours!* He hadn't gone far when he saw some **cattails** growing near shore. "Yes! Food!" he exclaimed. He'd been on the lookout for cattails ever since he read about them in Gramps' book. Nearly every part of the plant was edible. The inner part of the shoots were tasty and could be eaten raw or cooked, the roots too. And their pollen, shaken from the tail-like spike, could be used as flour to make pancakes. Now this was a find, a real find! It was hard, muddy work pulling out the stems, but ohhh, it was worth it. *Delicious, like sour cucumber!* He thought.

Cattails

He camped by the bay, built the fire high, and wrote in his journal:

June 30, Day 5 alone,

I'm happy I'm finding food. I can't believe I'm such a good hunter! I have Gramps' book to tell me what's edible. Right now, I'm eating cattails, but I'd give anything for a burger. But I'm okay. This is really hard, but kind of exciting too. I'm seeing new things every day and there's no one here to tell me what to do! Sorry, Mom, didn't mean it that way. At first, I was afraid of being alone, especially at night. But now that I have my spear, I'm not so scared. Did I say it has a real stone point? I think you all would be proud of me.

Love you, Mom. Love you, Dad. Justin.

PS. I miss Gramps and hope he's okay. I think about him all the time.

The following morning, Justin gathered more cattails and processed them for eating. Then he packed up and continued on his path around the bay. The distance was barely half-of-a-mile, but it took him nearly two hours to walk it because the shoreline was swampy and choked with vegetation, and as usual, there were dozens of downed trees to climb over. It was also very hot and buggy. Not the mild-mannered mosquitoes he was used to, but evil little **black flies** that attacked with a vengeance. Thank God he had a head net—he'd go insane without it! But his unprotected arms, legs, and back were red and bloody. He wished he had a net that covered all of him. He hated these flies. He just hated them!

Black flies, *which are about the size of a grain of rice, are the most hated pest in the north. They breed in the fast water of rivers. They have tiny mouths, so you may not feel them bite, but they leave a bloody wound that may swell as large as a tennis ball. Luckily, they don't fly well in wind, so a breeze will usually keep them away.*

As soon as he reached the river, he tore off his clothes and went for a swim. *Sweet relief!* The water was bitterly cold, so he stayed just long enough to wash off the sweat and blood. When he came out, the flies were gone. There was a nice breeze, which he figured had blown them away. As he was drying off in the sun, he noticed what looked like a yellow and red boat pinned against a rock downstream, about 10 feet out from shore. The open end faced upstream and was filled with water. He walked closer and jumped for joy when he discovered it was their canoe! "The Canoe! It's the canoe!" he hollered. "I'll make it. Now, for sure, I'll make it!"

The water was shallow—maybe two feet deep—and the current was slow, so he thought he could wade out and easily retrieve it. This proved more difficult than he expected. He could get to the canoe, no problem, but he couldn't move it. He pushed and pried, pried and pushed. Nothing, not even a budge! He thought the water-filled boat must weigh **a ton!**

He was ready to quit when he remembered a cartoon they were shown in science class. A cave man was able to move a huge boulder with a heavy pole, which the teacher called a "lever." He said levers made work easier. There was even a formula to calculate how much easier. *Maybe all I need is a lever!* Justin thought. It was worth a try, so he cut a thick pole from a tree near the water's edge and maneuvered it under the canoe. He pushed up, and the harder he pushed, the further the canoe rose and the faster the water drained. Suddenly, the canoe slid free off the rocks. Justin grabbed it and pulled it ashore. "Thank you, caveman!" he exclaimed.

He checked the canoe for damage. The yellow waterproof spray cover was still attached, but it was badly torn. One seat and two thwarts—the cross-braces—were broken and there were deep gouges in the **Royalex** skin. Otherwise, the canoe seemed sound. The packs were gone, but the aluminum tube that held Gramps' fishing pole was still tied inside the canoe, as were Justin's spare paddle and **bailer**, which Gramps had made by cutting off the bottom of a plastic jug. He pulled the fishing rod from its case. It was perfect! There was even a lure, which Gramps called a "jig", attached. Gramps had brought more lures, of course, but they were in a pack that was lost to the river.

He set up camp on a low hill by the river and spent the next few hours fixing what he could on the canoe. Then, he fished for a while. He didn't get a single strike, which frustrated and confused him. In a burst of anger, he cast the lure out as hard and far as he could. The jointed rod tip flew off into the water with it. He stared at where they had broken the surface. When he yanked the rod and started to reel in line the lure caught on a rock. He pulled and pulled but couldn't get it free. It was locked in solid.

*Almost a **ton**. The water in a filled canoe can weigh more than 1500 pounds!*

***Royalex** is a strong, thick plastic. Royalex canoes are almost indestructible. Unfortunately, they are no longer made.*

*A **bailer** is a plastic scoop used for bailing accumulated water out of the canoe.*

He knew that if he lost the jig, he would have to go back to fishing with a diaper pin and cloth. That worked, but only on fish like northern pike whose teeth slanted backwards. The jig, with its strong, barbed hook, caught *every* kind of fish! That was really useful, and he really, really wanted it back! He sat down and held his head in his hands. *What to do?* He soon realized that he would have to swim for the lure. He tied the pole to a tree so he wouldn't drag it into the water when he followed the line to the lure. Then, he stripped off his clothes, jumped in, and swam out. He found it and released it, and *awesome!* The rod tip was still attached to the line. When he returned to shore, he reminded himself to control his anger in the future. He also promised to be more careful how he fished and where he fished.

By now Justin was tired and ravenously hungry again. He had run out of cattails and had failed to catch any fish. His stomach was growling—he couldn't remember ever having been so hungry. He scoured the area for food but could find nothing. He was about to quit looking when he discovered a small patch of brilliant red, spike-like flowers growing in an open area near his camp.

He had seen flowers like these earlier, when he and Gramps were canoeing. Justin wasn't interested in flowers, but to keep the peace, he let Gramps tell him about them. Gramps called them **fireweed** and said they were one of the first plants to bloom after a forest fire. He said the leaves and shoots, which were rich in vitamin C, could be eaten raw or cooked. He added that the leaves made a tasty tea, and promised that before their trip was done, he would brew some up.

Fireweed

Justin gathered some shoots and leaves and ate them. The shoots were bitter but edible, but he thought the greenish-yellow tea was slightly sweet and delicious! Before he went to bed, he wrote in his journal:

July 1, Day 6 alone,

Hooray! I found the canoe today. It was stuck on a rock and I used a lever to pry it off. It was hard. I fixed some broken parts. I fished, but I didn't catch anything, and I almost lost my lure. I made some fireweed tea. It was great! I'm HUNGRY!!!!! I'd give anything for some real food, even Mom's stew, which I hate. Going to bed now.

While Justin was brewing **fireweed tea**, Henry was roasting a goose. He had been netting fish when he spied a large Canadian Goose on shore about 50 feet away. It was big—enough for several meals, and his mouth watered at the sight of her. He needed

Fireweed tea was very popular in Russia until about the 17th century, when Chinese traders began exporting tea.

this goose, badly! He drew the pistol and aimed at the center of her body—a head shot would waste less meat, but it would be easier to miss. *Bang!*

At the shot, the goose lunged forward and fell into the water. It flopped violently and struggled to swim, but it was too badly injured to go very far. Henry rushed into the water and chased after it. He grabbed it by the neck and the goose was his. He carried the large, limp bird to the place he had shot it. There, snuggled in the brush was a nest with five hefty eggs. He rejoiced that tomorrow he would have eggs for breakfast, his belly would be full. Still, he was sad that he had killed the mother goose and taken her eggs. If he hadn't needed food so badly, he would have left her alone. *The wilderness is a hard place,* he thought to himself as he walked away.

CHAPTER 11 — THE CANOE

Justin was harshly awakened by a swarm of mosquitoes that had come out of nowhere. They were biting his face and back, his arms and legs— everywhere! He had to get out of here. In minutes, the canoe was packed and ready to go. As he was loading up, he recalled Gramps' stern warning to always tie everything into the canoe so it would stay put if they capsized, and to coil the bow and stern lines and stow them under the elastic cords on deck. This way, they wouldn't snag the canoe or you in a capsize. He said there was an old navy saying, "Loose lines and a rough sea don't mix!"

When all was secure, Justin put on his lifejacket and prepared to paddle. He was about to push off when he realized that when he was with Gramps, he always paddled in the bow, or front, of the canoe. Now, he would have to do the job of both the bow- and stern-man. But where to sit? In the canoes he had seen in movies, the lone paddler sat in back, known as the stern, and set his gear near the front, called the bow. So, Justin did the same. He noticed that the bow of the canoe was about two feet higher than the stern, but no matter, he was sure that the movie way was the right way.

The current was slow and there were no obstacles to avoid—he just drifted and dreamed. Gramps had taught him the two most **important bow strokes**—the draw and cross-draw. The draw moved his end of the canoe towards his paddling side; the cross-draw moved it away. He knew there was more to canoeing than this, but he figured these two strokes were enough to get him downriver.

*Three **important bow** strokes are illustrated in Appendix 4.*

The river soon opened into a small lake. There was a nice tail wind and the canoe sped swiftly across the waves. Ahead was a tiny island. He tried to steer around it, but the high bow acted like a sail and kept the boat heading straight down-wind. No matter what he did, the canoe kept going straight—the bow strokes he had learned were useless in the stern of the canoe. Then he capsized with a splash!

He held on to the swamped canoe and let the wind carry them to shore. The water was very cold, but surprisingly, he wasn't. Maybe it was the warmth provided by his woolens and life vest, or perhaps it was just the flush of excitement. Either way, Gramps was right, he was sure glad he was wearing his PFD. In any case, he didn't want to capsize again. He would have to figure out this canoe thing before he continued on.

He missed the island and washed up on the far shore. As soon as he landed, he made a fire and brewed some tea. The wind was picking up and the sky was darkening, so he decided to camp, even though there was barely room to pitch his tarp here. The site was thick with trees and well protected from the wind, though, and there was plenty of firewood. It would do.

His thoughts turned to food, not that they ever fully left how hungry he was. He tried fishing by his camp, but the wind spoiled his casts. Finally, after 100 casts or so, he caught a fish. It was only about eight inches long, not much, but it was food, and much better than fireweed leaves! He couldn't understand why Gramps had said the fishing was so good in Canada. Except for that first day by the falls, he hadn't caught much. He didn't dwell on it, though, and quickly gutted the fish, then ran a green stick through its body and held the fish over the flames like a hotdog. When it was done, he devoured it completely, even the head. *I can't believe I did that!* he thought, knowing full well that he would do it again if there was another fish. It had been a nice appetizer, but he remained hungry.

The lake continued for about 200 yards from camp, then it narrowed to a slot the width of a canoe-length. Justin was curious about the narrows, so he walked over for a closer look. He brought his fishing pole, thinking the fishing might be better there.

Woah! It was a falls—a big falls—and unlike the one where he and Gramps had found the aerodrone, it was strangely **silent**. There was a sheer, vertical drop of about 30 feet—a canoe wrecker for sure. Justin couldn't understand why the rushing water was so quiet. An experienced paddler would see the broken horizon line that marked the drop, an inexperienced one would not. Justin knew he wouldn't have,

*The shape of a falls and the rocks below it, affect the sound of the rushing water. Many falls flow **silently**, which is why paddlers must learn to identify "horizon lines" where the water falls over the horizon.*

and was sure that if he hadn't capsized, he would have gone over the falls and all would be lost. He teared up; maybe Gramps was watching over him after all!

A well-used portage skirted the falls and the short rapids below it. Justin planned to check out the turbulent water, but first, he wanted more fish. He had learned that fishing was usually good below waterfalls, and that falls were often found where the river narrowed. He should have gone to the narrows immediately, not wasted time fishing near camp, but now he was where he needed to be and there was plenty of time to catch more fish.

He dropped his lure into a quiet eddy below the falls and started jigging. Thirty minutes passed without reward. Frustrated, he cast his lure into the current and let it flow downstream a way before he reeled it in. He had barely touched the crank on the reel when,

Arctic Grayling

wham! He had a fish, and boy, was it a fighter! It leapt high into the air, again and again! The reel screeched loudly as the running fish took line.

Ordinarily, Justin would have thought this was fun, but right now, he was too focused on food to care. He needed that fish! Ultimately, the fish wore out and he hauled it in. It was a beautiful, silvery-red color, with a high dorsal fin that resembled a sail. Justin thought it must be some sort of **sail fish.**

*The "**sail fish**" was an **Arctic Grayling**. Grayling are distinguished by their high dorsal fin, which resembles a sail. They are very entertaining to catch.*

He put the fish on a stringer and tried again. Soon he had two more fish. They were small, but together, they would make a fine meal. He remembered that he had been neglecting his photos, so he snapped several pictures of himself proudly posing with his fish. Then he re-started the fire and grilled the fish. He gobbled down two and saved one for later.

Satisfied for the night, Justin gathered more wood and piled the fire high. Sitting there, staring into the flames, eating fish and drinking firewood tea, he was pulled from relaxation by movement in the distance. He grabbed his spear and stood up for a closer look. It was a bear—a young black bear! It was about 100 feet away, partially hidden behind a bush. Justin froze! He was scared, even more scared than he had been with the wolves, but Gramps had ranted about bears so often in the past, that he knew what to do. The question was, could he do it? Gramps had met dozens of bears on his canoe trips—some so close that he could smell them. But there was never a serious problem.

Gramps said the solution was to talk to the bears—really! He tried to convince them that messing with him was a bad idea. Humans, he said, communicate mostly with words; animals rely on body language. What you say to the bear means nothing, how you say it is everything! Speak calmly but firmly, don't talk or act threatening.

He also said that bears are smart, much smarter than dogs. They won't pick a fight they think they could lose, but they are also bullies— if you act afraid or your voice shows fear, they'll take advantage. The trick is to watch the bear's ears—if his ears are up, he's listening, trying to figure out your intentions. If his ears go down, watch out! He's mad and may charge. And if you are attacked, fight back! Fight until the last breath—do not play dead with an aggressive black bear!

He also offered this advice, "Bears respect size. Small bears are afraid of big bears, and big bears are afraid of bigger bears. So, try to make yourself look bigger—stand on a rock or set a pack on your head." When Justin argued that the dumbest bear could tell the difference between a tall person and one standing on a rock, Gramps disagreed, firing back, "Think what you like, but I can say from experience, they can't!"

The wheels were turning in Justin's head. What to do? What to do? He didn't want a fight, but he didn't want the bear to have his last fish either. So, he stepped up on a big rock and clung to his spear. Then, he began a conversation. The bear's ears were up—he was listening! Justin spoke, "Hey, bear; you are a little bear, probably about the same age as me in bear years. Sorry you can't find food—but you're not getting mine! Tell ya what. I won't hurt you if you don't hurt me. But I got this spear here and a hatchet too, and you're gonna have to come through the fire to get at me. So, tell me, bear, whatcha wanna do?"

Suddenly, the **young bear** crouched down behind the bush. Seconds later, it popped up again. This strange up-and-down behavior continued for about a minute. Finally, the bear had had enough—it turned and ran away as fast as it could go.

*This is common behavior for a **young bear** that has just been "kicked out of the house" by its mom.*

When the bear had disappeared, Justin took a long, deep breath and melted to the ground. He felt a flood of warmth flowing back into his body. He was high on success! He couldn't believe, just couldn't believe, that he had talked to a bear and it had run away. He cursed himself for not taking any pictures. No one would ever believe he'd faced down a bear without proof. If he had some photos and an internet connection, he would upload them right now—and for sure, they would go viral. *What a rush!* Gaming was fun, but it wasn't real. This—this was real! He fantasized that if Sara had been here, she would have kissed him and thanked him for protecting her.

The wind was getting stronger and the sky was packed with clouds. It looked like rain—a long, heavy rain. At first, he had hated this campsite because it was small and snuggled in the trees. But now, as he watched them swaying all around him, he was glad that he was here. Before he went to bed, he did his chores.

First, he prepared for morning by gathering firewood and placing it under the tarp, making sure there was dry tinder and kindling so that

65

he could start a fire quickly. He also filled an empty food bag with water and put it by his bed. Next, Justin secured camp for the night. He checked the canoe, knowing it must be overturned and tied to a tree, then made sure the spear and hatchet were handy in case he needed them in the night and that the possibles pack was closed up tight. He thought about adding extra storm lines to the tarp—Gramps always said you can never have too many storm lines—but declined.

Shortly after he finished his chores, it began to rain. Gently at first, then harder as the wind picked up. It got colder, fast! He could see his breath when he exhaled. He checked his thermometer—42 degrees and dropping. It stabilized at 36 and the rain turned to snow and sleet. *It's the second of July!* He couldn't believe it was snowing, but they were far north. Oh well, it had been a long, hard day and he was ready for sleep. He crawled into bed and wrapped the yellow canoe cover around him; it would add some warmth and repel any rain that blew under the tarp. Still thinking about the bear, he was too keyed up to sleep, and in case he died he was anxious to write about how he scared it away.

July 2, Day 7 alone,
My 4th day on the river. A huge, like HUGE bear came into camp today and I was all alone, just me and my spear. I talked to him, yeah, talked to him, just like Gramps said in his book. The bear stood up and growled at me, then when I talked, it hid in the brush. Finally, it got scared and ran away. Good thing too, because I had my spear! I'm going slower than I thought. I think I've only come about 12 miles. 12 miles in 4 days. I gotta go faster. This canoeing thing isn't so easy. But I think I'll go faster after I figure it out.

He smiled contentedly and fell asleep to the whoosh of the wind and the patter of snow, dreaming he was eating a burger and fries. Sometime during the night, the snow changed to icy rain. The rain continued through the next day, and the next, and the next!

Justin remained hunkered down, but his stomach rumbled—three small fish in three days was not enough! There was nothing left in the possibles pack. He felt weak and light-headed and his ribs were beginning to show. He wanted to fish—had to fish—but he dared not go out and risk hypothermia.

He continued to read Gramps' book, hoping to find answers. He had never dreamed that there was so much to canoeing and camping! There was a passage about canoes that gave three important lessons. The first was that the **center of gravity** of a canoe should be situated

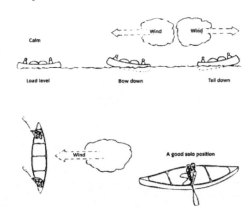

The Center of Gravity of a Canoe

appropriate to conditions. Canoes paddle best when they sit level in the water. A high end can act like a kite and capsize the canoe. The exception is when there's a headwind or tailwind. The end facing the wind should be weighted slightly down to prevent the canoe from "weather-veining" or turning broadside to the wind against your will. It followed up noting that a solo paddler should sit or kneel in the middle of the canoe—kneeling is more stable—because the middle provides the better stability and control than being in an end. In calm water, it's okay to sit in the front seat, facing backwards. And finally, it warned not to attempt rapids until you can paddle forward and backwards in a straight line, turn the canoe quickly right and left, slide it sideways around obstacles, and cross a fast-moving river without slipping downstream.

Justin studied the maneuvers—and noted the movies were wrong! He decided that when the sun came out, he would practice the new skills on the lake by his camp and wouldn't go down-river until he could do them all well.

Justin had another gnawing concern—he didn't know his exact location. He knew he'd been going roughly west, and that he was camped in a narrows, above a falls. But there were a lot of narrows and falls along the river. The question was, which one was he at? He turned on the GPS and paged to the map. Again, just dotted lines and two numbers, **357400 E and 5476200 N**. He hoped the book would explain what the numbers meant.

It did. He learned that points on a map are usually defined by their **latitude and longitude**. The numbers are given in degrees, minutes and seconds, which make them difficult to plot on a map. Gramps preferred the Universal Trans Mercator (UTM) coordinate system, which is much easier because it uses the gridlines on the map for reference. He plotted the numbers and connected them with lines and for the first time in 11 days, he knew exactly where he was at. But he was shocked to discover that the falls below his camp were marked as a rapid on the map! He learned an important lesson—maps aren't always accurate!

When Justin realized he was located at mile marker 74—and that the big lake, with the great fishing, was just 19 miles away—he let out a holler! If I can master this "canoeing thing" so I won't crash in a rapid, he thought, I'll be there in a day—that is, if I can find enough food to keep me going! Then he shut his eyes real tight and wished that Gramps would be there waiting for him.

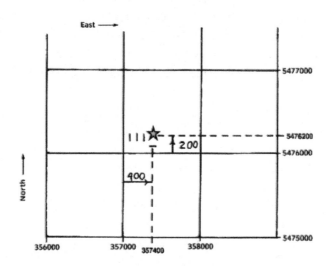

The UTM Coordinate Location of the Star
is 357400E and 5476200N

CHAPTER 12 — THE SLINGSHOT

The rain quit at noon and a blazing sun flooded the sky. It had been three days since Justin had moved from this spot. Mother Nature had grounded him, perhaps for paddling without doing his homework, much like when he was grounded for not prioritizing school. At least at home he didn't have to fight to stay warm and dry. Here, it was a constant battle.

He stretched and looked out at the new world around him. Everything looked different—much different. Before the storm, the lake was about 25 yards from his camp. Now it was at his doorstep. A big rock that had been on shore was now under two feet of water! His camp was surrounded by downed trees that looked like piles of match sticks. *Lucky they missed!*

For a moment he just stood there dazed, surveying the damage. Then suddenly, he screamed, "Canoe!" He ran to where it had been tied. Luckily, it was there, still tied to the tree—half tipped, half submerged—but it was there! *Where's the paddle!* Justin couldn't see it, was it still inside the canoe or lost in the rising waters? "Please be there, please be there!" he pleaded, as he righted the canoe. Yes! It was there, trapped under the seat.

He knew he was lucky it hadn't floated out and vowed in the future to pull the canoe higher up on shore and to keep the paddle in camp, not with the canoe. Justin was learning new things every day. And he was learning them fast!

The crisis averted, he prepared to go fishing. He needed food badly, so he grabbed his pole, slingshot, and spear, and headed to the falls. He arrived to find the river very different. What earlier had been a quiet falls, was now a roaring cascade that sprayed mist like a shower. And the once-gentle rapid that followed now boiled with huge rooster tails that stood as high as he did! The quiet eddies where he had fished were gone—washed out by the high water. The river had also been crystal blue before the storm. Now it was brown and cloudy. No way could he catch fish here!

What to do? What to do? He leaned against a tree and hung his head, weary with hunger. For nearly two weeks, he had survived— thrived even—on his wits and what he had learned from Gramps' book. Now he was backed into a corner and the flooded river threatened to take it all! He needed energy to paddle and portage, and he had none.

A narrow portage trail that ran for about 500 yards skirted the falls and the rapid below. Gramps had written that the portages on remote rivers were often kept open by animals who, like people, had to get around obstacles like rapids and falls. "Study the ground and you'll see their tracks," he wrote. Justin brightened slightly at the thought that if he walked the trail slowly and quietly, he might see a bird or rabbit or ground squirrel. If not, perhaps he'd find a good fishing spot in the quiet water below the rapid.

Justin walked slowly and stopped frequently to look and listen. When he stopped, he froze in place and cupped one hand to an ear so as to better hear the slightest sounds. He was learning to separate the noises of plants from the patter of paws. He was becoming a hunter!

Justin was pleased to discover that, except for a short section near the end, the trail was all downhill. He couldn't carry the 75-pound canoe, but he could drag it. Parts of the portage were flooded, too, enough in some places to float a canoe—that would make dragging easier. The flooded portage was one good thing that had come out of the storm. He added it to his options, but his first priority was food. After that, he would consider his next step.

Surprisingly, Justin didn't see a single animal—not even a songbird or field mouse—along the portage. And there were no clear eddies at the base of the rapid, so fishing was out of the question. No pity party this time, no time to wallow. His spirits lifted as he recalled a western movie he'd seen on TV. An Apache boy about his age went alone into the wilderness to "seek a vision." He had water but no food. When he returned to his tribe ten days later, he shared his vision with the elders. They were so impressed that they honored him as a warrior. Justin figured that if that boy could go ten days without food, he could too. The river would drop in a few days and he could fish again. He would survive—no, thrive—he was sure of it.

He was ambling back to camp when he saw a **grayish-colored bird** that was about the size of a small chicken, sitting motionless in a tree, about 10 feet away. The bird sat perfectly still, not moving a muscle. Cool and quietly, he loaded his slingshot and took aim at its breast. *Wham!* The bird came down, flopping violently, and he instinctively stepped on it.

"Meat!" he hollered, as he claimed his prize, "I got meat for supper!" Momentarily, he felt a twinge of sadness that he had killed the bird in such a violent way, but he needed food, and the thought quickly passed. What now? He would roast it over the fire, of course, but first he figured he would have to pluck the feathers. He hoped that wouldn't take too long.

Back at camp, Justin proceeded to do so. He plucked and plucked and plucked some more. Thirty minutes passed and he was still plucking! His patience broke and in an instant, he grabbed the bird by the legs and swung it hard against a tree. The back of the bird flew into the forest; the meaty body remained in his hand, attached to the legs. At first, he was stunned by what happened, then a big smile flashed across his face. He

Justin saw a spruce grouse. Spruce grouse eat evergreen needles and perch in tree. They are hard to see because they sit perfectly still even when humans come within a few feet of them. For that they're often called "fool hens" because they are so tame. They are very good eating! To quickly clean upland birds like grouse and pheasants, step on the wings and pull upwards on the legs. The meat will separate from the skin and feathers cleanly.

couldn't believe he had just butchered the bird by smacking it against a tree! He thought, *if I get another bird, I'll just step on the wings and pull on the legs!*

He cut off the wings and legs and plucked the few straggling feathers. Then he skewered the body with a green stick and roasted it over his fire. He impatiently watched the bird as it cooked, the smell teasing him. The longer it cooked, the better it smelled. His mouth watered—he'd seen dogs salivate when they ate—and he wondered if he was becoming more dog-like and less like a human!

Twenty minutes later, the bird was done. With trembling hands, he cut off a piece. *Oh my God, it's awesome!* he thought. It was moist and tender, tasted like chicken—but better than any chicken he'd ever had. It was, well—*amazing!!!* He was sure he had never eaten anything so wonderful in his life.

The bird wasn't very big. He could easily have eaten it all. But he ate just half, savoring each bite, chewing thoroughly, licking his lips. He imagined he was watching TV. A large banner that read *Amazing!* kept rolling across the screen. He couldn't get that word out of his head.

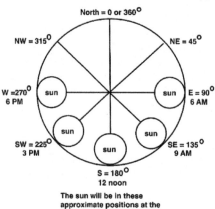

How to Use Your Compass as a Watch

Justin wanted to know the time and he didn't have a watch, but that was no problem, since Gramps' book told **how to use your compass as a watch.** It was easy, you just take a compass bearing on the sun and compare the bearing to a diagram in the book. The sun rises in the east and sets in the west, so the bearing will change with time.

Justin got 225 degrees, or southwest. That would be about 3PM—too late to pack up camp and portage. Besides, he needed to perfect the canoeing strokes described in Gramps' book before he continued on. He decided he would practice paddling for a few hours. Afterwards, if he was still ravenously hungry, he would slowly eat some of the bird. His mom often scolded him for eating too fast. She said he would feel less hungry and his food would digest better if he ate slowly. Anyway, it was worth a try. He wanted to save some meat for breakfast so that he'd have energy to start the day.

Justin put the rest of the bird inside an empty freeze-dried food bag. He built a small house of rocks and put the bag inside the house. He hoped this would prevent animals from getting his food while he was out on the lake practicing. After he had secured his food, he put on his lifejacket and paddled out into the lake to begin the hard work of learning a new skill.

Justin was focused, like he used to be for his games. He knew that if he screwed up in a rapid, he could lose the canoe and all his stuff, maybe even his life! So, he studied the diagrams in the book and tried to duplicate them exactly. He learned fast! By the end of his session, he had mastered the most important maneuvers. He was able to turn the canoe smartly right and left, slide it sideways around obstacles, paddle forward and backwards in a straight line—all without switching his paddle from side-to-side. Justin was surprised that he could do so much with just a handful of paddle strokes.

He likened it to horseback riding. A few years ago, his dad took him to a horse show where the horses did cool tricks. The skilled riders made the tricks look easy. Perhaps canoeing was like that too. *Maybe you can make a canoe perform like a well-trained horse, if you know what you're doing!* Justin thought. If you don't know what you're doing, the best canoe in the world won't prevent you from capsizing in big waves or crashing in a rapid. Gramps constantly hammered his philosophy that "knowledge and skills are more important than gear." Justin had become a believer!

As Justin was preparing for bed, *Is Gramps dead?* Crossed his mind. He pushed the thought away, but there sure were some spooky things going on. Why was he always able to find food—not every day, but often enough to keep him alive and fit for traveling? Why didn't a tree fall on him during the storm when so many came crashing down around him? There was almost no chance he would find the canoe after it went over the falls, yet he found it and was able to repair it. Why didn't his paddle float out of the over-turned canoe when the water rose by his camp? How, after three days without food, did he just happen to find a dumb bird sitting in a tree, let alone kill it? And spookiest of all, was finding a book that contained everything he needed to know in order to survive. Surely someone from another dimension must be watching over him.

He teared up. *Gramps.* He was sure it was Gramps! He blurted out, "Gramps! Gramps, wherever you are, thank you for taking care of me. I love you! I love you. Sorry I was such an asshole, I'm not like that anymore, you'll see!"

Then the tears fell away, and he drifted off to sleep.

Shortly, he awoke. He'd been dreaming, but he couldn't remember about what. He looked around the forest. It was dark and quiet. The only noise was the soft sound of waves lapping against the shore. A week ago, he would have thought it spooky. Now, darkness, silence, and solitude didn't bother him at all. He built up the fire then took out his journal and began to write:

July 5, Day 10 alone,

The water is muddy, and the portage is flooded. The fishing is awful! I shot a big bird with my slingshot and cooked it up. It tasted better than any chicken I ever ate. Sorry, Mom, your chicken is good too. Can you beam me over some right now so I can compare? Crazy. I'm starting to understand why Gramps loves this stuff. I worry that Gramps might be dead, but I have a feeling that he's not. God, I hope he's alive! I'm writing this in the dark by the fire and I'm not scared at all. I wonder why? I keep trying the satellite phone. Still nothing! I hope I can figure it out before the battery dies. Going back to bed now.

CHAPTER 13 — TREASURES

Gramps was very much alive! He was doing fine, though he was still terribly upset about Justin. He'd been living off of ducks and geese and fish and lily tubers. Just the other day, he shot a big, fat rabbit. He had run out of water lily tubers, and since he missed vegetables, he hiked back to the pond to get more. While he was there, he decided to check out the airplane more thoroughly—it might contain some stuff he'd missed—something he could use to build a boat.

It did. He was thrilled to find a duffel bag that contained a sleeping bag and **closed-cell foam** sleeping pad, a down vest and acrylic stocking cap, a nylon tarp, a large roll of duct tape, a set of dining utensils including fork, knife, and spoon, a can of Dinty Moore beef stew, and a candy bar. Naturally, everything was soaking wet. The sleeping bag, tarp, and stew were his most precious finds. *Stew for supper!* He couldn't wait to crack that can!

He also discovered a small zippered bag inside the airplane, which contained an assortment of tools including wrenches, screwdrivers, and a hammer. He had no immediate use for the tools, but he took them anyway, thinking they might come in handy. While he was rummaging around, he found a cargo net, too, that had been disconnected and was floating, and a long, thick rope that was used to dock the airplane. The net could be used for fishing and though the rope was too thick and heavy for camp use, he could unravel it for cord.

There are open-cell and **closed-cell foam** *sleeping pads. Open-cell pads are like a sponge; they absorb water when they get wet. Closed-cell pads have sealed cells so only the outer surface gets wet. Open-cell pads are more comfortable, but they're not waterproof.*

He removed another airplane door to use as a sled, and he missed having a comfy backrest in camp, so he took the back seat. With the doors and seats gone, light flooded into the fuselage and he was better able to see what remained inside— or rather, what didn't. Gone was the emergency locator beacon that is usually kept in the tail of the aircraft. It must have either floated out or been taken by the men in the helicopter. Wedged in back was a melted blob of metal that Henry thought might have been the aerodrone.

Before leaving the float plane, he took one last look at the two decaying bodies that were still strapped into the front seats. Fish and other small organisms had been biting the bodies; their once pink flesh was chalky-white. Short flaps of skin fluttered in the water like the pectoral fins of a fish. The eyes of one man had been plucked out and a finger had been eaten. The smell of rotting flesh permeated the cockpit. Henry smiled, *Wonderful karma!* he thought.

While he was gathering lily tubers, he spotted a big, fat beaver swimming slowly along. He waited quietly until he could get a good shot and then bang! he again had food. Henry leapt into the water after the beaver and swam it to shore. He was thrilled, figuring that the beaver was enough for several meals, and though he hated to kill the beaver, it was a lot of meat! He remembered a quote by the famous American painter, George Catlin:

"…we are invited by the American Indians to feasts of dog's meat, as the most honorable food that can be presented to a stranger and glutted with the more delicious food of beaver tails and buffalo tongues."

From Letters and Notes on the Manners, Customs and Conditions of the American Indians — Mouth of the Yellowstone, 1832. George Catlin was born in 1796 and died in 1872. He was the first white man to describe and paint the natives who lived in the western United States.

Henry tied all of his treasures to the sled and dragged them back to camp. There, he skinned and cleaned the beaver and cut the rich, red meat into strips. He set the strips on a rack of green sticks above a smoky fire. He figured it would take about eight hours to smoke the meat. During that time, his primary chore would be to keep the smoky fire burning. In between tending the fire, he reclined in his new chair. *Ahh, how wonderful to have a soft backrest,* he thought. Then he opened the can of stew and put it on the coals to heat, using his new metal spoon to stir the stew. Back home, a spoon had no value; here, it was a cherished possession. The stew would be ready soon—the thought of which made his mouth water.

*A **Bull Boat** is a small round boat commonly used by American Indians and trappers. The frame was made from bent saplings, which were tied together and covered with buffalo hide or canvas. These awkward boats were incredibly slow, but they were very light (about 40 pounds) and could carry several hundred pounds of gear. A good team could build one in a day! Men on the Lewis & Clark Expedition built bull boats and used them to float down the Yellowstone River after their horses were stolen.*

His thoughts turned to Justin. How was he? Where was he? He took a long, wondering look upstream. Then, he teared up and thought out loud, "That boy is tough. He's doing fine. I feel it in my bones." When the stew was hot, he dived in. It was delicious! And, after it was gone, the empty can would become a handy mug.

He went to bed that night thinking about Justin and about building a boat so that he could paddle upstream and find him. He had a waterproof tarp, duct tape, and cord. A canoe would be too complicated to make, but a small **Bull Boat** would be relatively easy— that is, if he could find the rest of the necessary materials. It would be very slow, of course, and it would be impossible in wind, but it was a boat! He thought that if the weather cooperated, he could probably build one in a few days. He would start on it tomorrow!

Bull Boat

77

CHAPTER 14 — A BIRTHDAY TREAT

Justin was up at the crack of dawn. He re-started the fire, made some fireweed tea, and ate the last of the bird. Then he packed up camp and started to portage. At first, he dragged the canoe by the handle at one end. He pulled and pulled and pulled and pulled. It took him 30 minutes to go 100 yards! He was wearing himself out and getting nowhere fast. There had to be a better way. He grabbed the bow line at the front and pulled the canoe behind him, like a dog on a leash. The tight rope cut into his hand, so he quickly abandoned this method. Then he remembered a picture he saw of a man pulling a rickshaw.

There was a horizontal bar at the front of the rickshaw. The man leaned against the bar and pushed. *Aha! New plan.* He removed the canoe's stern line and tied it to the bow. Now there were two ropes attached to the bow. He cut a thick pole about three feet long and tied a rope to each end of the pole. Then he leaned into the bar and pushed. *Success!* The canoe moved slowly along.

An hour later, he was hot and sweaty and covered in mud, but he had completed the portage. The sun was up, and the day was warming fast—it would be a scorcher. Mosquitoes were out again in droves, biting him everywhere. He had to get out of the woods fast! First to cool off and clean up, though. He put on his **lifejacket**, then he jumped into the water, clothes and all. He stayed in just long enough to wash off the mud and stink. Minutes later, he was in the canoe, drip-drying and floating downriver.

When he was well out from shore, he felt a light breeze and the bugs disappeared. As he drifted, he listed to himself what he'd learned about bugs. He remembered them coming out in force just before and after a storm, and that they quit biting when the storm began. He figured that was because they must not fly well in wind; he planned to camp on a breezy point rather than a deep in a forest in the future. Them had seemed to disappear when it got cold, too, now that he thought about it, and they came back when it was warm. Black flies had also seemed to stop biting when they got stuck under the tarp, instead climbing to the top, trying to get out; mosquitoes weren't so kind, continuing to bite whether inside or out of shelter.

Gramps had also told Justin that bugs were attracted to navy blue and black clothing, and that light colors attracted them least. When Justin asked why so much gear was the wrong color, Gramps replied, "Because most people don't go into the deep woods, and many of those that do, don't have a clue that color counts."

The current was slow but determined, so for a time, Justin just floated quietly along, his eyes constantly on the prowl for something edible. There were birds and turtles, that was all. He'd heard that turtles made good soup and wished he could snag one, but whenever he got close, it would dive and be gone.

*Experienced paddlers often wear their **lifejackets** when they swim. Reasons include:*

1) You float high— your feet don't touch sharp rocks on the bottom.

2) It's easier to swim, especially in wind or currents.

3) If you practice swimming while wearing your lifejacket, you'll know how to react in a capsize.

He studied the map and found that he was at mile 77, with just 16 miles to go. If all went well, he'd be at the "terrific fishing" spot today. *Tasty, delicious fish,* He could taste them, lots of them, and huge ones! He imagined grilling them on green sticks or roasting them from a tripod. Maybe he would pin them to a plank and broil them before a fire.

He thought about having all the fish he wanted, any time he wanted, not needing to ration what he ate so he'd have food for later. All he had to do was wet a line, and seconds later, he'd have fish, more fish than he could possibly eat. *Sixteen miles.* The fish market was just 16 miles away! He estimated that he was doing about three miles an hour. At this speed, he'd be there in time for supper—or sooner, if he dug in and paddled hard!

Justin was hot, very hot. He was down to his T-shirt and cooking in the noon-day sun. His thermometer read 83 degrees. *Eighty-three!* He couldn't believe it was that warm after it snowed just days earlier. The blinding sun made it difficult to see the river ahead—which could be very dangerous in rapids! His eyes hurt from constant squinting and he wished he'd had sunglasses.

A trick from the book came to mind. Gramps had written that the Eskimos carved snow goggles from caribou bone or wood. They cut thin eye slits in the goggles and tied them to their face. The book said that **duct tape sunglasses** could be made much the same, all that was needed was to, "Stick two pieces of tape together—sticky-side to sticky-side—and cut slits for your eyes. Punch a hole at each end of the tape and tie a cord to each hole. Then tie the goggles around your head." *Good idea*, thought Justin.

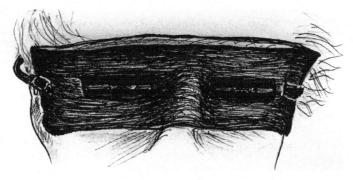

Duct Tape Sunglasses

He put ashore on a gravel bar, then he got out the duct tape and made sunglasses. When he had finished, sweat was dripping from him. He couldn't stand the heat any longer, so he stripped off his clothes and dove into the water. He paddled around for several minutes, then crawled ashore and washed his clothes. Afterwards, he took a nap.

He awoke three hours later, surprised that he had slept so long. It was still early in the day, though, and he'd made good time, so he decided to stay a bit longer and fish. Cast after cast after cast yielded nothing. Not so much as a bite. Gramps had written on the map "No Fish Here" and there weren't! He thought, *Gramps was right—again!*

His clothes were dry, so he put them on. Clean body, clean clothes. He felt great! His mom had washed his clothes hundreds of times and he had never once said "Thank you." That would change when he got home. He promised that the next time he wrote in his journal, he would thank his mom for washing his clothes, and for all the other nice things she did for him.

Before he pushed off in the canoe, he checked the map again. He saw that the river narrowed at mile 79. *Drat!* There was a rapid and another portage. But he was on the home stretch, it would be what it would be.

For about 30 minutes, he just floated happily along, carefree and proud of his progress. Then, in the distance, he heard the roar of rushing water. The closer he got, the louder it got. Soon, he saw dancing white plumes that indicated a rapid. He canoed to the left shore, stopped, and studied the map. Gramps had indicated portages on the map with a *P* and had detailed the route with a dashed line, but there was no *P* by this rapid, which suggested that it might be canoeable. Then again, maybe not. Gramps had warned that not all portages were marked, and some that weren't marked still bypassed bad rapids! You wouldn't know until you looked at them.

A quarter-of-a-mile west of the rapid, there was a *P*. The dashed line ran for 500 yards and cut off a long loop in the river. Justin groaned at the distance. He figured it would take him a full day to drag the canoe that far. *No use complaining until I check it out, though,* he thought.

First, to find the portage. He scanned the shoreline for an opening in the trees or a slight dip in the vegetation. Either could indicate the location of a portage. He saw neither and so would have to compute a compass bearing from his location at the mouth of the river to the portage. His compass read 320 degrees. Before he read Gramps' book, he would have followed that 320-degree bearing and probably missed the portage. But now he knew that portages and hiking trails weren't always plotted perfectly on maps, so precise compass headings didn't guarantee success.

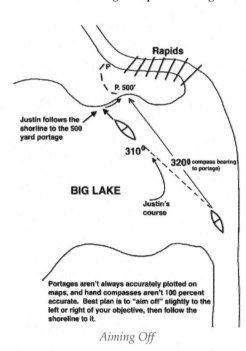

Portages aren't always accurately plotted on maps, and hand compasses aren't 100 percent accurate. Best plan is to "aim off" slightly to the left or right of your objective, then follow the shoreline to it.

Aiming Off

Gramps had written, "One degree of compass error equals 92 feet per mile of ground error. So, if you are going one mile and your compass bearing is off by four degrees, a reasonable amount with an **orienteering hand compass,** you will miss your objective by 360 feet, or about the length of a football field!" Justin estimated that the portage was about a half-mile away, so he changed his compass bearing to 310 degrees, which is slightly west of 320 degrees. Then he followed the 310-degree bearing. When he hit shore, he turned east, to his right, and followed the shoreline to the portage. The book called this procedure **aiming off.** Justin thought it worked real slick!

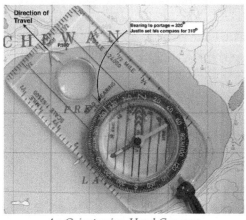

An Orienteering Hand Compass

He found the portage easily, even though it was obscured by trees. *If only Gramps could see me now!* He thought with pride. Justin pulled the canoe ashore—well up on shore—and tied it to a tree. He checked the knot by pulling on it to be sure it was secure. It held! A clearing large enough for two tents and a small stone fire-ring revealed that others had camped here before. It was getting late, so he decided that he would camp here too.

Before making camp, he decided to walk the portage to see how difficult it was. Naturally, he would bring his slingshot and spear—he had gotten into the habit of taking them everywhere he went. In the western movies he had seen, the American Indians always had their weapons with them. He thought that, like him, they were always hungry and looking for food! And when they found it, they were prepared! As he was leaving, he remembered that his pack and paddle were still in the canoe. He took them out and set them by a tree where he planned to pitch the tarp. Then he turned the canoe over so it wouldn't catch the wind or fill with water if it rained.

At first, the trail was fairly level and easy to follow, then it climbed and meandered through a thick stand of evergreen trees. It went up and down hills, turned left and right, became narrower and narrower, harder and harder to follow. "Whoa!" said Justin as he stopped in his tracks. He'd been lost on a portage before and he didn't want to repeat the experience!

He turned and went back to a place that he could recognize. He tied his red bandanna to a bush to alert him to the difficulty ahead. Then he cautiously continued on, stopping every 50 feet or so to **blaze a tree** with this knife. Blazing was slow work, but the alternative was getting lost on his way back to camp. As he walked and blazed, he questioned his hasty decision to portage the rapid without first looking at it. Gramps had written, "It's always wise to check a rapid before you carry your gear around it. If you can canoe or line some parts, you'll save yourself a lot of work." Justin knew he should probably portage. Still, he wanted to look at the rapid, just in case it was canoeable.

*To **blaze a tree**, you cut a handful-sized piece of bark off the trunk. This exposes the light-colored wood inside. However, cutting through the bark provides a pathway for insects and disease. Blaze trees only in an emergency! Colored plastic ribbon (available a most hardware stores) is easier to see than a blaze and it doesn't harm the tree.*

Justin smiled when he saw sunlight streaming through the trees— it often indicated the end of a portage was in sight. It was, and shortly he was at the river. He took a long, cool drink of water and washed his face. Then he turned and headed back up the trail. He had barely gone a dozen feet when he saw a porcupine. It was standing motionless by a tree and didn't seem at all concerned that he had a spear and was just a canoe length away.

Gramps had told him that porcupines moved so slowly that they were easily killed with a club or rock. Gramps had never eaten porcupine, but he knew others who had. They said that the lean, dark meat tasted like duck, but better—and that the liver was especially sweet and tasty. Gramps emphasized that the American Indians would kill a porcupine only as a last resort—if they were starving and couldn't find any other food.

He said he once shared a campsite in Saskatchewan, Canada with natives who were working for a survey team. The company had provided fresh pork chops, potatoes, and salad, flown in by bush plane, for supper. Still, one of the young men killed and cooked a porcupine.

The man's father was furious, and he cursed his son for killing the slow-moving animal, and that he had broken a tribal taboo, one that their ancestors wouldn't be quick to forgive. He said, "Porcupines are for when you're starving to death, and we aren't starving!"

But I am! He thought and killed the animal with a thrust of his spear. The porky was fat, he guessed about 20 pounds. That was enough meat for several days, if it didn't spoil. He figured he'd roast the animal and eat his fill. Then he'd smoke the remaining meat over his campfire. Right now, though, his big concern was how to get his kill over the portage and back to camp without being stuck by quills. After some thought, he decided to tie a cord around the animal's neck and drag it. The walk would take about 10 minutes—time enough for him to think about what to do next.

Justin had no idea of how to clean a porcupine. The only animals he'd ever cleaned were a bird, which had feathers and a fish that had scales. This animal had long, barbed quills! He knew he had to slit the belly and remove the internal organs, but how to do it without getting stuck? When he cautiously rolled the animal on its back to expose the belly, it flopped over on its side, and its legs closed. He tried placing thick sticks between the legs to hold them apart while he cut, but the sticks would slip. Momentarily, he just sat there, wondering what to do. Then, suddenly, he got a bright idea and remembered, *KISS*. It was a slang abbreviation for the rule of thumb, "Keep It Simple, Stupid."

His plan was ingeniously simple. He tied the porcupine to a tree—stretching a rope from one front leg around the tree to the other front leg, and likewise back leg to back leg, with its back facing the bark. This exposed the soft belly but not the quills. He smiled smugly and thought, *I'm one smart kid!*

Next step after removing the internal organs was to skin the animal. But again, how? No way was he going to touch a quill! He decided to first burn off the quills, then skin it. He built a hot fire and set the porcupine on a rack made from thick sticks. The **quills** burned off surprisingly quickly. His original thought was to skin the animal right after the quills burned off, but now, *Singeing off the quills is a good, safe way to cook a porcupine in the field. American Indians have used this method for centuries.*

as he watched—and smelled—it cook, he decided to let it roast where it was until it was done. Then he'd remove the skin.

When the porcupine was done—after well over an hour—Justin removed it from the fire. He started to use a forked stick and his knife to remove the skin, but it peeled off easily, like the skin on broiled chicken.

He cut a small piece and popped it into his mouth. It was delicious, unlike any meat he'd ever had. He'd never had duck, though, so he didn't know how it compared. As he gorged himself, he fantasized about what his friends at school would say when he told them he had killed and eaten a porcupine.

"What did it taste like?" asked one.

"Uh, like duck, but better," he answered.

"What's duck taste like?" asked another.

"Like porcupine, but not as good." He cleverly replied.

Justin stayed up late that night, tending the fire and smoking the meat. He remembered that his dad's tasty spareribs took about six hours to smoke. He thought that because the porcupine had been thoroughly cooked, two hours would be enough. To pass the time while the meat was smoking, he wrote in his journal. In the middle of a sentence, dropped his pencil, and exclaimed, "Oh my God, it's July 6. My birthday! I'm 14!" The excitement quickly vanished when he realized that Gramps wasn't there to share this special day.

Instead, two gnawing questions ate at his mind. First, Gramps always checked rapids before he portaged them. And until now, so did he. This portage was a long way from the river. *Did Gramps guide me here?* And second, he was tired and ready to camp when he arrived. Still, he grabbed his spear and slingshot and walked the long portage trail. He just happened to be in the right place at the right time to see the porcupine. *If I had come a minute earlier or later, might the animal have been gone?* He mused about it in his journal:

July 6, Day 11 alone,

Happy Birthday to me! Where's the cake, Mom? I need cake! Today, I used my compass to find a portage and I blazed trees so I wouldn't get lost. I wanted to check the rapid before I portaged it, so I hiked to the end. Before I could scout, though, I found a surprise, a porcupine! If I had ran the rapids, I would have missed it. Gramps wrote that porcupine tastes a lot like duck. Can we have porcupine and duck together some time so I can tell which one is better?

PS. Thanks, Mom, for washing my clothes and all the other nice stuff you do for me.

He thought again about the porcupine. More now than ever, he was certain that Gramps was watching over him and that the porcupine was a birthday gift from him.

Gramps was definitely watching over him. He had started to construct the Bull Boat, but things weren't going as fast as he hoped. He had to travel far from camp to find saplings that were just the right size for the framework. He also had to make a paddle—and for that, he needed thicker wood. His dream of completing the boat in a few days now seemed impossible, but he'd just have to keep plugging away until it was done, then he'd rush upriver as fast as he could paddle!

CHAPTER 15 — YES, I CAN DO IT!

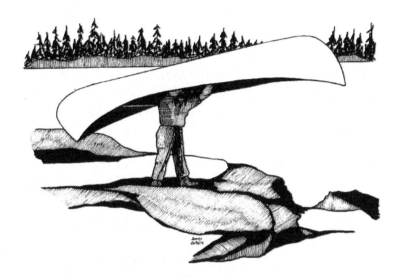

Justin fell asleep tending the smoky fire. When he awoke, it was nearly noon and the fire was out. He panicked momentarily, thinking an animal had taken the porcupine while he slept, but it was untouched and still on the rack above his fire. He cut a strip of meat off the carbon-black carcass and popped it into his mouth. He thought it tasted like the burned, smoked turkey thigh he once had at a picnic. Still, it was wonderful!

He cut the meat into strips and carefully sealed them inside the giant plastic bag he pulled from the possibles pack. Then he walked to the edge of the lake to greet the day. The wind was up and blowing hard, with yard-high waves on the lake. He wanted to paddle to the rapids to see if it was canoeable, but the wind was too strong. He decided that since he was stuck at the portage, he might as well just do it. It would take hours to drag the canoe across, so he'd best begin now.

He cut a thick pole from a tree again and attached the two bow lines to it. Then he snuggled against the pole and pushed. For a while, the canoe slid smartly along. Then came the forest with its bumpy up-and-down trail and he was stopped dead in his tracks. Justin sat down on a log to think.

He remembered that for many years, his grandpa had outfitted and guided canoe trips for teenagers. Most of his trips were co-ed. If you wanted to get his dander up, all you had to do was suggest that a fourteen-year-old was too weak to carry a canoe. He'd flash back with, "A fourteen-year-old boy or girl can easily carry a 75-pound canoe a quarter-of-a-mile with a smile on their face and a song in their heart—if the boat is set up right—which meant having a comfortable carrying yoke with cushy pads that are spaced to fit teen shoulders!"

All of the carrying yokes on Gramps' canoes had **moveable shoulder pads** so that they could be moved closer together to fit narrow shoulders or farther apart for wide shoulders. Justin thought that if other kids his age could carry canoes, he could too. At any rate, he had

to try. He thought the hardest part would be getting the heavy canoe onto his shoulders. Gramps could do it alone, with a single motion, but Justin would need some help.

He turned to a trick he'd seen when he was eight while canoeing with Gramps. A young

Canoe Yoke with Moveable Shoulder Pads

woman was preparing to portage her solo canoe. She picked up the bow end, and in one smooth motion, turned the canoe belly-up and set the bow on a thick branch that was about as high as her. Then, she walked under the canoe and then backed into the padded yoke. *Slick, real slick!* Justin thought as he copied the procedure, seconds later under the yoke.

He immediately discovered that the pads were set for Gramps—too far apart to fit Justin's shoulders. He loosened the wing nuts and moved the pads closer together. Then, with grit determination, he started down the winding trail. The canoe was heavy, very heavy. His shoulders hurt, his knees wobbled, and he dripped with sweat. Mosquitoes bit his back and there was no way to swat them. The pain grew like a mountain, and the mountain grew higher with each step he took. But he was carrying the canoe, alone, by himself. "Yes," he muttered, "I can do it. I can do it!" Indeed, he did, and without stopping once to rest.

The end was less glamorous. Gramps would have set the canoe down gracefully, but Justin just threw it off his shoulders. Fortunately, it landed on some bushes and not a rock. Dazed, he ambled to the river on rubber legs and plunged into the cold, clear water. Almost instantly, the pain was gone. He came up laughing, numbly chattering, "What a rush! What a rush!" Then he took a long drink of water and sprawled out in the sun to rest.

He was drifting off to sleep when he remembered that his paddle, spear, and possibles pack were still sitting by the trail where he had left them when he picked up the canoe. He would have to go back for them. In any case, he was full of life and didn't mind the walk.

It was late afternoon when he finished the portage, and the wind was still blowing strong, so he decided not to continue on. He still had a long way to go and was worried that canoeing alone was much slower than canoeing with Gramps, especially in wind. He remembered how confident he'd been at the start, thinking that a 200-mile walk through the wilderness would be easy, and how thrilled he was when he found the canoe and thought that now he had it made. Still, there was a good chance he would get there on time. Gramps had written that if you wait for a time-window when the weather is right, you can make up lost time. To get there on time he would need just such a window. Right now, though, he needed rest. So, he rigged a hasty camp, ate some meat, and wrote a quick journal entry.

July 7, Day 12 alone,
Eleven miles to go to the big lake with good fishing. I should get there tomorrow if it's not too windy. Then, it's 169 miles to the airplane. If there aren't a lot of rapids and portages, I should make it in time.

CHAPTER 16 — MOOSE!

Justin was awakened by the blazing sun shining in his eyes. He sat up to find a picture-perfect day, the kind you dream about but seldom get. *A window!* He staggered to the river and washed his face. Then came breakfast—cold, smoked porcupine, washed down with river water. He packed camp quickly, excited to get going. After all, the big lake was just 11 miles away. It was possible he'd get there today! He loaded the canoe, put on his lifejacket, and paddled out to greet the day.

The river was beautiful—cobalt blue and crystal clear. He could see the bottom, which he judged was about six feet down. There was a slight breeze, just enough to keep the bugs away, but not enough to slow his progress. The current was quick, though thankfully, there were no rapids. So, for the next hour he just drifted and dreamed and watched the shore-line slip by. He was curious about his speed, so he turned on the GPS. It read 3.2 miles per hour. He was thrilled that he was going so fast, and without even paddling! *Just a few hours to the lake!* He rejoiced.

Shortly, he entered a tall canyon that had a huge nest in a crag on top. Two bald **eagles**—a white-headed adult and a brown-headed juvenile—were soaring above the nest. The young bird was flying close to the nest, poorly, probably unsure of its new wings. Its parent was

Eagles often use the same nest every year, making them bigger each time. A typical bald eagle nest is about five feet in diameter, and a record-sized nest in Florida measured nine feet wide and weighed three tons! Young eagles have mottled brown heads, taking up to five years for them to turn white. The bald eagle got its name from the word "Balde," which once meant "white."

Moose are fast, having been clocked at 35 miles per hour, nearly as fast as a kangaroo! An adult moose stands taller than a horse and weighs about 1500 pounds. Bulls during the rutting season, and cows during calving season are especially dangerous! If you see a moose in the woods, quietly walk away.

flying protectively overhead, encouraging its young to fly. Justin had seen pictures of bald eagles in school and on TV, but this was the first time he'd seen them for real! It was quite a thrill.

He continued to drift along, soaking up the scenery until the current slackened and he had to paddle. Around the bend, the river narrowed, and the current picked up again. He was focused on navigating a small rapid when, he came upon a **moose** just ahead. No, two! A cow and her calf. They were blocking the narrows, pre-occupied with something in the water. Justin back-paddled hard and the canoe slowed slightly. The calf was less than 150 feet away; if it didn't move soon, he would hit it! He remembered Gramps saying that a cow moose with a calf was dangerous. They would charge if pressed, and that though moose looked slow and awkward, they were actually quick as lightning! Justin was closing fast.

"Moose!" he yelled at the top of his lungs. "Moose! Moose, get out of the way!" But his cry was drowned out by the noise of the rapid. Now he was 50 feet away. He yelled desperately, *"Moose!"* again, and this time, he loudly slapped the water with his paddle. The moose snapped her head up, looking straight at him, fire in her eyes! Then suddenly, in perfect unison, the pair turned and ran. In seconds they were out of sight.

Justin's hands were shaking. His body was shaking! There was a small gravel beach on the right. He paddled to it and put ashore. Then he sat down cross-legged on the beach, meditation style, wondering what would have happened if the moose had charged.

Once again composed, Justin continued down the river. For another hour, there were no scary interruptions. Then, the river narrowed and curved to the right, and he heard the sound of rushing water. Another rapids! He checked the map. No portage was indicated, but by now, he'd had enough experience to know that portages weren't always marked—or at least accurately marked—on maps. Gramps' book offered this important tip about how to find unmarked portages:

"More often than not, you'll find portages on the inside bend of rivers. For example, if the river curves right, the portage is probably on the right; if it curves left, look left. Why? Because it's shorter to follow the inside of a curve than to go around the outside. If in doubt, always check the inside bend first."

The rapid curved to the right, so Justin paddled to the right shore. He tied the canoe to a tree then went to investigate. Almost immediately, he found the portage, which was more of just an animal trail. *The rapids might be runnable,* he thought, since the trail didn't look like it was used very much. If it was, he'd save a lot of time and energy. Gramps always took his paddle with him when he checked out rapids. He used it like a third leg, for stability when he walked. Justin preferred his spear, which he could also use to kill dinner!

Justin walked along the rapid and studied it from every angle. There was a ledge at the top where the water made a sharp drop, but it was broken away near shore—he could easily **line the canoe** through the broken part. The rest of the rapid looked easy, if you knew what you were doing. Justin wasn't sure he did, so he thought it wise to line or portage.

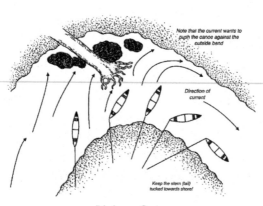

Lining a Canoe

Note that the current wants to push the canoe against the outside bend

Direction of current

Keep the stern (tail) tucked towards shore!

Lining was fast and easy. Attach a rope to each end of the canoe, then use the ropes—which Gramps called lines— to guide the canoe around obstacles in the water. Lining was also dangerous—one mistake and the canoe could swamp or capsize—so being extra cautious was important!

Ordinarily, he and Gramps would line the canoe together. Justin would hold the bow line; Gramps would take the stern. Gramps would yell directions like, "Let out some line, or pull in a little!" Gramps also emphasized that the stern must always be closer to shore than the bow; he said, "If the stern swings out beyond the bow—even a little bit—the current could catch the canoe and turn it side-ways, then capsize!" Justin decided that the safest plan was to control the canoe with a single stern line. That way, he wouldn't have to worry as much about where the bow was going.

He held the rope tightly and eased the canoe into the current. It slid easily over the ledge and through the narrow passage. It was moving fast, fast enough that he had to run along shore to keep up. Several times, it got stuck on rocks and he had to wade out and push it off. He was getting the hang of it, even thinking it was fun. Extra fun because now he wouldn't have to carry the brain-draining canoe over the portage! Minutes later, the canoe was safely at the bottom of the rapid. He snubbed it to shore and looked upstream where he'd begun. "I did it, I did it!" he beamed loudly, then he set his camera on a boulder and took a selfie with his canoe and the rapid in the background.

When he'd finished, he jumped aboard and paddled on. It was getting late, and he decided to camp. *Where to?* The shoreline was choked with vegetation—and probably bugs. He wanted a **sun-lit spot with a breeze** that would blow them away, but places like this were hard to find. Hard enough that often, he'd have to paddle for hours just to find an opening that was large enough to pitch his tarp. Gramps had emphasized that most accidents happen when people were tired. Well, now he was tired and there wasn't anywhere to camp.

As the sun set and he figured he'd have to paddle into the night, an opening appeared in the forest. He paddled over to it. A campsite! There was a nice flat tent spot—two, in fact. And lots of dry wood on the ground. He was hungry, so he decided to eat before he set up camp. He rummaged in the possibles pack for the smoked porcupine. When he found it, he deliberated, *What shall I have for supper? We have cold, smoked porcupine, hot smoked porcupine, and hot and cold smoked porcupine.* He set the package down and looked into space. "Too many choices, I just can't decide!" he called out with a grin.

A Sun-lit Spot with a Breeze

Then he went back to rummaging, looking for the cup. *Where's the Sierra Cup?* He shuffled through his gear. "Where the hell is it?" he said aloud. He looked and looked but couldn't find it. He thought about when he had it last, remembering that he'd been in a hurry that morning—that instead of packing it away, as was his custom, he just hung it from his belt. He'd seen paddlers in the Boundary Waters carrying Sierra Cups that way, so he hadn't given it a second thought. Now he looked down at his belt, the cup was gone. *Gone! No!* Horror of horrors. How could he have been so stupid as to hang it from his belt? Without the cup, he had no way to heat water — no way to make fireweed tea.

Or did he? He remembered a documentary he'd seen about the stone-age. It showed a woman dropping hot stones that had been heated in a fire into a clay pot filled with water. The more hot stones she dropped in, the hotter the water got. Eventually, it boiled! He didn't have a clay pot, but he did have a strong freeze-dried food bag, which he thought would work just as well. But heating water this way would be slow and time consuming, there had to be other options.

Justin thought some more and remembered a demonstration in science class. The teacher said he would boil water in a paper bag. Everyone laughed, but sure enough, he did! He filled the bag with water and placed it inside a wire cage, only so it would keep its shape, then on top of a Bunsen burner. A few minutes later, the water boiled — the bag didn't burn! Everyone cheered!

Justin had wire—he could make a cage to support the food bag. Things were looking up. He smiled and called out, "Menu change! Hot smoked porcupine with boiling fireweed tea!"

That night he went to bed knowing that he'd reach the big lake the next day. He would catch all the fish he could eat, *more than he could eat!* Porcupine was good, but fish was better. As he was writing in his journal, he thought about Gramps.

July 8, Day 13 alone,

Gramps, why did we hang around the drone for so long? Why didn't we know it would be dangerous? If we'd just looked and taken pictures, then moved on, we would have missed the airplane and you would be here now.

CHAPTER 17 — THE FISH MARKET

Justin awoke to another beautiful day. The sun was barely up, and the temperature was already 80 degrees. It would be a scorcher. He wanted to know his exact location, so he turned on the GPS and nibbled on some smoked meat while it connected. He was thrilled to discover that he was at mile 87—the big lake was just six miles away! If there were no obstacles, he could cover that in about two hours. He studied the map, there were none marked! He rejoiced that it would be an easy float. He shoved off smiling, excited that he'd soon be there—good fishing was just hours away!

The time passed quickly. Five miles—four—three—two—and suddenly, the big lake came into view. He let out a holler of joy as soon as he saw it. On a long, sweeping esker high above, was the treasured campsite he had sought. It was just as the map notes described it—on the crest of a hill, with level spots for a dozen tents, and a south-facing view to catch the morning sun.

He pulled ashore and tied up the canoe, then scrambled up the hill to the campsite. A light breeze wafted through the sparsely spaced trees. Hooray, there were no bugs! A stone fire ring indicated that others had camped here before, but the ring had been washed clean by rain, so it probably hadn't been used for some time.

A large square of half-rotten plywood leaned against the fire-ring. Cut marks suggested it was used for cleaning fish. *Yes!* Another sign of good fishing. He thought this might be a fly-in fishing camp. Gramps had told him that people paid big money to fly into places like this where the fishing was good. Justin hoped a floatplane would land *right now* and rescue him, but he knew the chances of that happening were like winning the lottery without buying a ticket! He wasn't in the clear yet and survival was still his course of action.

He unfolded the map and traced his finger along the route to the end where he would meet the float plane. There were only eight marked rapids remaining, and most of the portages around them were short. He was thrilled to discover that from the lake on, it was all-river, no more lakes or bays to cross and wind wouldn't slow him down. He also observed that the river was narrower than before. This suggested that the current was faster. If so, he'd make better time. He smiled at the thought that he was ahead of schedule and could afford to take a breather here and stock up on fish—and any other food he could find—before he continued on.

He dropped the possibles pack then went out to explore. He hadn't gone far when he discovered a small trash dump hidden in the trees. Gramps would have gone ballistic if he found it, but he was thrilled! There was a lot of stuff that he could use including an assortment of aluminum pop cans, beer bottles, and a liter-sized plastic soda bottle; a rusty enameled steel pot with a tiny hole in the bottom; a bobber and tangled fishing line; a broken lawn chair; a pair of tennis shoes, one with a burnt toe; a 10-inch steel tent stake; and a heavily dented stainless-steel Thermos.

He set right to work. He washed out the plastic soda bottle and whittled a wooden plug for the mouth. Then, he tied a loop of parachute cord around the neck so he could hang the bottle from his belt. This would be his canteen. He sealed the hole in the pot with a small wad of aluminum foil, which he pounded flat with the back of his hatchet. He filled the pot with water, and it held! Now he could boil fish or fowl or brew a pot of fireweed tea. He tried on the tennis shoes. They were much too large, but they'd be great for camp. He filled the Thermos with water. It held, too! Now he could have hot tea any time he wanted! He broke off a leg from the lawn chair and flattened one end. It would make a handy digging tool. The list went on and on, he found a use for almost everything. "Sorry, Gramps," he called aloud. "Wherever you are, I can hear you ranting about this trash, but right now, I'm lovin' it!"

Justin spent hours improving his treasures, so consumed in doing so that he hardly noticed when it got dark. Too late to gather evergreen boughs for a proper bed, he just curled up on top of the lifejackets and covered himself with the canoe's yellow spray cover. Minutes later, he was fast asleep.

It was barely light when he awoke with a start. A strong, musty odor filled the air; there was an animal at the edge of camp, and it was munching on something. He bolted upright and recognized that the possibles pack was gone. The animal had it! It must have dragged it out from under the tarp. Now it was eating the food inside. "My food! He got my food!" he mouthed under his breath.

He slowly rose, spear in hand, and faced the animal. It glanced at him briefly then confidently went back to eating out of the shredded pack. Justin squinted and thought about what he was looking at. *Was it a small bear? A badger? No—it was a **wolverine**!*

Wolverines are omnivores, meaning they eat plants and animals, though they much prefer meat. Wolverine fur doesn't retain much water, so, unlike other furs, it doesn't ice up when it's cold. For this reason, it is prized for use on the hoods of winter parkas.

Justin knew about wolverines. Gramps had shown him pictures and told him stories of them. Like how they were powerful and cunning, and how they would attack animals that were much bigger than them—even bears! There was even a documented case where a wolverine had killed a polar bear! Gramps said that trappers hated wolverines because they cleverly robbed their traps. Gramps' words echoed in Justin's head. "Don't mess with a wolverine! If you do, he'll be eating you! If you see one, stand still and stay out of his way."

Justin did just that. He stood still and watched. The wolverine just kept on eating, seemingly oblivious to his presence. Occasionally, it looked Justin's way—checking that he hadn't moved. He didn't! When the wolverine had finished eating, it turned and slowly walked away.

As soon as the animal was out of sight, Justin collapsed to the ground. Strangely, he hadn't been scared. Alert and focused, respectful and ready to fight if attacked—yes! But not scared. He remembered how frightened he was when Gramps left. He was constantly freaking out, certain he would starve to death or be killed by a wild animal. But he hadn't died. He read Gramps' book and learned how to survive—thrived even!

101

When the wilderness canoeing plan had been first proposed, his mom was just as skeptical as Justin. She was certain that he would die or get hurt on the canoe trip—possibly eaten by a bear or wolf. Gramps just laughed. He said that was nonsense—she had seen too much TV! People always warned him that bears would eat him alive in Canada! Or when he paddled the Everglades, they ranted about deadly pythons! When he canoed the Rio Grande River, which divides Texas and Mexico, it was bandits and drug lords that would kill him. Gramps said not to worry—that the wilderness is safer than a city, if you know what you're doing. "And I do!" he emphasized. She smiled weakly and said "Okay."

Justin thought it strange that his mom hated canoeing and camping when Gramps loved it so much. Gramps had taken her many times when she was little, but she never liked it. Justin reflected on how, at first, he hated canoeing and camping too, and he took every opportunity to let Gramps know it. Now he had come to like it, maybe even love it. He teared up again and softly said, "Dammit, Gramps, why aren't you here? Why aren't you here? I think I have your genes!"

He thought again about the wolverine. It was hungry, just like he was. Yeah, it got his food, but he could get more. Just yards away, there was huge lake filled with tasty fish. At that thought, he grabbed the fishing pole—he was going there to get some now! Later, while his fish were cooking, he'd repair the possibles pack.

He walked out on a rocky point and cast his lure into the water. Immediately, the lure was hit. And it was a big hit! The fish took off running hard. It jumped and turned and twisted. The drag on the reel screeched loudly as the fish pulled powerfully away. Justin raised the rod tip higher and higher—he didn't want to lose that fish! Then, snap! The line broke and the fish was gone. Justin stood there, stunned with the realization that he'd just lost his only lure. He felt sad and defeated—he didn't know what to do. Then he remembered the big pike he'd caught on a strip of cloth and a safety pin. If he did it once, he could do it again. Maybe. He could make another hook but not another red bandanna. It was long gone—probably still hanging from a tree branch along the portage where he'd left it.

Suddenly, words from Gramps' book rang in his ears. "They'll bite on anything that glitters." Justin perked up; he knew exactly what to do. He cut a triangular piece of aluminum out of a soda can from the trash dump. He punched a hole in one corner of the triangle. Then he hung the shiny piece of metal on a hook that he had fashioned from a diaper pin. Justin rattled the lure. It glistened brightly in the sun! He was sure it would fool a fish.

Funny, he had gone from insanely happy, to super sad, and back to happy again in a matter of minutes. He remembered his mom telling him that this often happened to people, herself included. She called it being on an "emotional roller-coaster."

Justin tied on his new lure and went back to fishing. He got a hit on his second cast, but the fish got away. A few casts later, he landed a **beautiful fish**—a kind he had never seen before. It was spotted brown, with a light underbelly, and it was about 18 inches long—a nice eating size. He gutted the fish then grilled it on a stick over the fire. He thought it was as tasty as the pike, but it had fewer small bones, so it was easier to eat. As soon as he finished eating, he went back to fishing. Soon, he had two more of the speckled fish—more than he could eat!

*The **beautiful fish** was a **Lake Trout**. Average length is 24 to 36 inches. A record lake trout—caught with a rod-and-reel—weighed 72 pounds!*

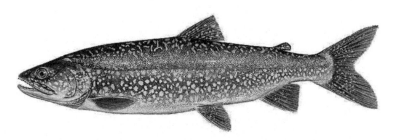

Lake Trout

July 9, Day 14 alone,

Gramps, you were right, the fishing here is great!!! Every time I caught a fish, I hollered, "Gramps was right! Gramps was right!" The river looks easier than before. There are no more big lakes to cross, so I think I'll make good time. I'm tired of being hungry so I'm going to stay here another day and stock up on fish. Oh, and thanks, Gramps, for the great map notes. I think I would be dead without them!!! I'm sorry I never told you that I think you're cool. But I'm telling you now!!!

CHAPTER 18 — THE SIGNAL FIRE

It was nearly 10 when Justin arose the next morning. He had awakened earlier, but he slept in because he could. He re-started the fire and boiled some water. A smile spread across his face, satisfied that there was no need to sleepily stagger to the lake to fetch water this morning—a full pot of it was sitting by his side! He'd filled the pot the night before. He marveled that at home, water was just a faucet-turn away. Here, it was a daily walk, and sometimes a long one. He missed home—Mom and Dad—and Sara. He wrestled with what to tell his parents when he was rescued, and they learned that Gramps was gone.

He decided that since he was staying here today, he would build a big log-cabin style signal fire, just in case he saw an airplane or some people. He would also set out his space blanket. *Not making the same mistake again!* He was concerned that the fire might spread into the forest, so he chose a rocky point where there were no trees or grass.

He built the fire slowly, carefully placing each stick so it would be in the heart of the developing flames. Gramps had written that bark doesn't burn as well as wood, with the exception of birch bark, so Justin split every piece he piled. He needed tinder, so he made some **fuzz sticks** and coated them with resin, which he gathered from **bark blisters** on a Balsam Fir tree. He arranged the fuzz sticks inside the log-cabin frame like a tipi, so they would concentrate the flames. When he was satisfied with his work, he set some fresh-

Fuzz Stick

Sometimes called "feather sticks", **fuzz sticks** are made by shaving thin curls from a dry piece of wood. One end of the curl is left attached to the wood. The thin curls catch fire fast!

Break a Bark Blister
The Resin Burns Like Kerosene

cut evergreen boughs by the fire. The green needles would smoke really well when he tossed them on the flames. He was ready to light the fire the instant he heard or saw an airplane.

Justin was putting the finishing touches on his fire when he saw a rabbit. It was about 40 yards away, sitting there, looking at him. His mouth began to water. Fish were good, but meat was better! He took a step towards the rabbit and it accelerated like a bat outta hell. *If only I had a gun*, he thought. But of course, he didn't. Now all he could think of now was trying rabbit. He couldn't get it out of his head. Gramps had eaten it many times, and he said it tasted like dark meat chicken. *That sounds delicious!*

Justin walked to where he had seen the rabbit and could see now that it had dashed up a narrow trail that went by his camp. The trail went under some low branches, so he guessed it was a rabbit trail. Maybe the rabbit would use the trail again. Maybe again and again. If so, perhaps he could trap it. But how? *Stop wasting time!* He snapped out of his rabbit-fantasy and thought, *Best get some fish.*

He grabbed the pole and headed to where he'd caught the other fish. He fished and fished and fished some more. Nothing. *What the hell!* Yesterday, he caught three fish here. Today, there were none. Then it hit him—it was late afternoon, the hottest part of the day. He'd fish later, when it was cooler. Meanwhile, he'd explore his new digs. He planned to walk the esker and maybe find some food along the way.

The esker opened into a small meadow that was packed with low bushes and **colorful wildflowers**. Justin never cared much about flowers at home, but here, he was quite taken with them. He wondered why. Perhaps they reminded him of his home in sunny California, or maybe it was the color they added to what was otherwise a mostly green forest? Justin broke off a flower and stuck it in his hat, then broke off another one and stretched out his hand. "This one's for you, pretty Sara." He played.

Dragon's Mouth, Common Burdock, Wild Columbine, fireweed, and Canada Thistle are some of the many **colorful wildflowers** *that grow in northern Canada.*

For a while, he just wandered through the meadow, touching and smelling the pretty flowers. Then, as he turned to go, he saw a low bush with some bluish-colored berries—*blueberries*! They were slightly green still and not very sweet, but they were edible. Justin gathered enough to fill his hat, then he headed happily back to camp.

He was surprised to find blueberries this early in the season; when he and Gramps canoed the Boundary Waters, Gramps made some fine pancakes with blueberries they had collected along a portage. Justin thought the pancakes were delicious—one of the few things he had liked about the canoe trip. When he asked Gramps if he would make them again this time around, Gramps said, "Probably not, it's well into August before blueberries mature." But he added that global warming or a long string of hot days could change that.

Justin went back to fishing as soon as it cooled off. He fished and fished, but still didn't get any hits. Just as he was ready to quit, he felt a light tug on his line. He reeled in a small one, about 12 inches long and speckled like the ones he'd caught the other day. It wasn't much, but he thought that with the blueberries he had enough for supper. Besides, he was tired of fishing.

As he was walking back to camp, he spotted the rabbit again. It was sitting on the trail in the same spot as before—and not at all concerned that Justin was staring at him. Justin looked at the rabbit and whispered, "I'm gonna get you, rabbit. I'm gonna get you." The rabbit sat rock still, just looking at him as if to say, "Don't bet on it!" Justin moved and the rabbit took off again. Justin knew he couldn't catch it, couldn't spear it, and probably couldn't hit it with his slingshot—maybe he could snare it. He'd never made a snare and didn't know how but there was snare wire in the possibles pack, and he was good with puzzles. *I'll figure it out,* he thought, and considered what to do while making supper.

After he had finished eating, he walked to where the rabbit had been sitting—wondered why it always stopped there. Either way it was not the place to set a snare. He figured the rabbit had to be running fast and through a small window and found just such a spot where the trail went under a low branch. The branch would be a good place to attach his snare. He formed a wire noose and put a slip knot at one end. Then he tied the wire to the branch. He adjusted the slip knot so that the loop was a bit wider than the rabbit. Finally, he set some sticks on each side of the snare so the rabbit couldn't go around it. He stood back and admired his work. "Maybe it'll work, maybe it won't," he muttered to himself.

Justin hustled back to camp with a new project in mind—to make a new spear point from the heavy steel tent stake he had found at the dump. The stone point was good, but steel would be even better! He set the tent stake on a rock and pounded it flat with the back of the axe. Then he sharpened it on a coarse rock. Sharpening went slow—it took more than an hour!

When he was satisfied, he replaced the stone point with the metal one, securing it with epoxy and snare wire, as before. When the spear was done, he felt the tip. *Sturdy and sharp!* He nodded enthusiastically. This was a real spear, a really real spear! He whooped and hollered, lunged into space, and pretended he was being charged by a bear. The bear was coming in fast! He stood rock still, shaft anchored against a foot, blade pointed at the rushing bear. He yelled, "Whoa, bear!" But the bear kept coming. It ran into the spear and was killed instantly. Justin rejoiced!

Play time over, Justin gathered more firewood and then nodded off after writing.

July 12, Day 17 alone,

I found some blueberries. Gramps said they wouldn't be ripe yet, but they sort of were. Saw some pretty flowers. I wanted to pick one and save it for you, Mom. And one for Sara too. But they wouldn't last. Fishing is okay, but not as good as Gramps said. Maybe it's too hot for fish. I don't know. A fish broke my line and I lost my lure. But I made another one from a soda can I found in the trash. There's a trash dump here and I found lots of stuff I can use. I don't have enough fish yet. I have to get more before I go on.

In the morning he awoke to another beautiful day. He'd been thinking about the rabbit all night and was anxious to see if he had caught it. If he did, there might be enough food for two days! He slipped on the burnt tennis shoes and headed to the snare.

Nothing. No rabbit, no wire. Things were disturbed though, and he shuffled through the brush to investigate. He lifted one branch, and, *Yes!* There it was, dead and half-hidden. He gently removed it and coiled the wire, then returned to camp.

Breakfast was a feast—grilled rabbit with blueberries. He thought the rabbit was delicious, maybe better than the bird. There was enough left for supper too. He thought about fishing—the rabbit would only last a day—but he was tired of fishing. He was tired of working, too, decided he just wanted to eat rabbit and hang out today. Maybe he would go for a swim and wash his clothes. He considered his desire to relax. *Don't get lazy,* he thought. The clock was ticking, and he had to be on his way. Reluctantly, he packed up camp and headed down the river.

In a bit of amazing coincidence, while Justin was eating his rabbit, Gramps was eating one too! He'd set some dead-fall traps along a rabbit trail and was catching them regularly. Like Justin, he had also built a signal fire—three of them, actually, and arranged them in a **triangle**. They were all primed and ready to go!

*Repetitions of three are a universal distress signal. Three loud noises in an even rhythm, whether whistle tweets, gun shots, anything, are widely recognizable. Similarly, rescue fires should be arranged in a **triangle** if possible and made to be very smoky.*

Henry built the signal fires after the boat that he had built crashed and sank during its trial run. He was about 100 yards from shore when it happened. A big burst of wind had blown the boat onto a sharp rock, and the delicate nylon skin tore—water poured in. Henry tried to swim the boat ashore, but he couldn't fight the strong wind and it was carried it out to sea, lost in the gathering flow. He swam ashore, terribly disappointed. Once again, he was a man without a boat.

CHAPTER 19 — GUN SHOTS

Justin was making good time on the river and thinking about how much he missed his parents and Sara, and of course, Gramps. He was sick of eating fish and birds and rabbits. He longed for burgers and fries, pizza, his mom's homemade chicken soup, and salads with lettuce, tomatoes, cucumbers, onions, and lots of thick dressing. He rolled his eyes—he could taste them now, and was surprised that he missed vegetables, he didn't like them at home.

Suddenly, he heard a muffled *bang!* It was followed by another *bang! Gunshots!* He was sure they were gunshots. They were coming from somewhere upstream, probably from the lake he had just left. Gunshots meant people, people on the lake! Should he continue on, or return to where he had camped?

He decided to turn back, and quickly. It was an opportunity for rescue. He spun the canoe to face upstream and paddled as hard as he could, but for every yard he gained, the current pushed him back a foot. He was going nowhere, fast! His chest burned. It burned more than when he had crossed the finish line after winning second place in the school track meet.

Just when he was about to give up, he remembered what Gramps had written about rivers—that the water flows fastest on the outside of bends and slowest on the inside of bends, and that in general it flows faster in the middle than near the shore. Justin angled towards the inside of the bend he was on and paddled close to shore. *Gramps was right!* The current was much slower there. Canoeing upstream had suddenly become a whole lot easier!

Thirty minutes later, perspiring heavily, he arrived back at the big lake. He headed towards the sound of the shots. He thought the shooter must be fairly close, probably **within a couple miles.** The lake was cluttered with small islands to canoe around. Easy enough—he just followed the twisting shoreline and avoided them. Thirty minutes later, he had cleared the islands and was heading into open water, pushed along by a gentle breeze. It was hot and sunny, so he just sat back and ruddered and let the cool breeze push him along. Every few minutes, he called out, "Help! Help! Help me, I'm alone!" There was no answer.

*Sound carries farther over water than on land. The shooter could have been more than **two miles** away!*

Bummed that he had backtracked all this way and didn't find the shooter, he angrily put ashore to rest. He took a short swim, then a nap. When he awoke, the lake was dead calm—ideal for paddling. He figured that if he left now, he would be back at the river and on his way to the float plane in an hour. But the sun was low in the sky, and he didn't want to paddle in the dark, so he used a procedure from Gramps' book to **calculate the approximate time to sunset.** He fully extended his arm, then he turned his hand sideways. He counted eight fingers between the sun and the horizon. Each finger equals about 15 minutes of time, so sunset would come in about two hours. Justin thought that would be more than enough time to make it back to the river before dark.

He turned on the GPS and charted his route to the river. *It's getting late, I'll cut through the islands and save some time,* he thought, rather than paddling around them like he did before, but since navigating a lot of narrow passageways in failing light could be tricky, he decided to keep the GPS running while he paddled. This would use precious battery

Calculate the Approximate Time to Sunset

time, of course, but he thought that was better than getting lost. He noted that the GPS bearing was 92 degrees, or nearly due east. He set 92 degrees on his compass for quick reference—and as a back-up—just in case the GPS went down.

Forty minutes later, he reached the islands but became confused. The directional arrow on his

GPS pointed straight through the nearest island, not between them. *What should I do? Return to the main shoreline or stick to my plan?* He chose the GPS. Gramps' book made it sound like navigating by GPS was easy. *Well, it wasn't!* He kept running into dead-end channels. It was a maze, a dark, confusing maze! It had taken him barely 30 minutes to follow the shoreline around the islands going west. The run back through them took an hour!

*Lightning may jump a dozen feet or more across water, so don't snug up against the shoreline if you're boating in an electrical storm. Instead, keep within the **cone-of-protection** offered by the shoreline trees.*

He was about half-a-mile from the river when **lightning** flashed across the sky. Justin knew that a canoe on open water was a perfect lightning rod. He had to get to shore fast! But he also knew that lightning tends to strike the tallest thing around—often a tree along the shoreline. And sitting under a tall tree in a storm is not a good place to be, either!

The common advice in a lightning storm is to leave your shelter and seek a low place away from tall trees—then wait there until the storm has passed. This could mean standing out in the rain all night! Sitting up on an insulated pad is a more practical plan. Justin sat on the foam-filled life jackets.

Gramps had written that a **cone-of-protection** extends from the top of the tallest near-by thing, whether trees, earth, or rock, about 45 degrees outward towards the water— and that the safest place to be was inside this cone-of-protection. Justin quickly headed towards the nearest land. When he was about 60 feet from shore, he stopped paddling. Then he waited there for the lightning to pass. A few minutes later, it did, and he continued on.

Hungry, tired, and pissed off that he hadn't found the shooter then got lost in the islands, he put ashore on a rocky point not far from his old campsite. He was too tired to fish, so he just pitched the tarp and went to bed. He was dozing off when lightning again lit up the sky. Minutes later, there was a cold blast of wind and the rain came down. White lightning danced in the sky—it was a frightening show! Justin sat up and pulled his knees in tight. Gramps had told him that if lightning strikes the ground near you and you are lying flat the electric shock could stop your heart. "Better to sit up and burn your feet and butt than to fry your heart!" he emphasized.

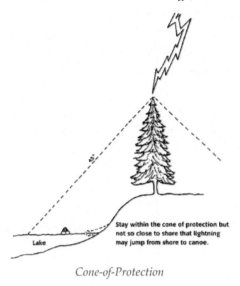

Stay within the cone of protection but not so close to shore that lightning may jump from shore to canoe.

Lake

Cone-of-Protection

The storm passed, and Justin went back to bed. He tried to sleep, but his mind was focused on food, and the constant work of getting it. He laughed at the thought that he could have chosen summer school over this grueling canoe trip. If he could do it over again, he would prioritize school! Then he'd be at home, eating well, sleeping well, watching the tube, and playing with his friends. And Gramps would be there, too. He was weary from the work it took to survive. He wanted to go home, now!

CHAPTER 20 — THE SATELLITE PHONE

Grizzly Bear!

Justin was up with the sun. First, catch breakfast, then get on the river and push hard to the float plane. Today was July 14. The plane would come on July 22—eight days from today—and it might come early in the morning, so he'd best be there a day ahead, on the 21st. Canoeing 169 miles in seven days would be tough, but doable—that is, if he kept finding food. He had to have food to paddle! He washed his face and drank some water, then he grabbed his fishing rod and spear and walked to a weedy inlet where he thought there might be fish. He hadn't gone far when he saw a bear. It was a big bear—a very big bear! It was cinnamon-colored and had a small hump on its back. It was a **grizzly bear!**

Justin stood there, frozen with fear. His mouth was dry, his heart was pumping; he was too frightened to say a word. Gramps had told him that bears communicate almost entirely by body language—that they may attack if you act afraid. Justin knew that if he said anything, there would be fear in his voice. So, he just stood there, dead silent, his spear pointed at the bear. He recalled how, earlier, he had whooped and hollered and flashed his spear at an imaginary bear that invaded his camp.

But this bear was real! And huge! He felt very small and very weak. He wanted to run, but he knew better. The bear was eating something and didn't seem too interested in him, so he slowly and quietly began to back away. The bear just kept on eating. As soon as the bear was out of sight, Justin bolted for the canoe and pushed off into the water. He paddled out into the lake, hoping the **bear** wouldn't **swim** after him, and it didn't, luckily. He waited about an hour, then he cautiously went ashore. The bear was gone, but his fear wasn't.

Bears are good swimmers, easily able to swim several miles across a lake, so camping on an island is no guarantee you won't run into them! They are fast runners and have been clocked at nearly 40 miles per hour! And the myth that bears can't run fast downhill is just that—a myth—you just can't out-run a bear!

He melted to the ground and sobbed. *Enough!* He had had enough of this harsh land, enough of constantly trying to survive. *I want to go home, now!* His pity-party was interrupted by the sound of a muffled *bang*. Justin was certain it was another gunshot. It was as distant as before, and probably fired by the same shooter. He thought about paddling out to find the shooter but decided that, like last time, it would be a waste of time. Then he remembered the satellite phone and decided to try it again.

"Dammit all, I gotta make this thing work," he said under his breath as he pushed the start button. Seconds later, he was greeted by a "low battery" signal. *No, no, no!* His last lifeline began to fad and panic was creeping in. "No! Now I'm really screwed!" he screamed and watched the screen go blank as the phone died.

His temper flared and he cocked his arm like he was getting ready to throw a baseball. Then he remembered the spare battery, hidden under a flap of foam inside its waterproof box. He lifted the foam and took out the battery. Underneath it was a business card that read:

Alex Youngquist
CANOE NORWAY
75 22 00 90
U.S.: 011+47 75 22 00 90

Justin studied the card. He wondered if 011 was the prefix he needed to call home. He installed the new battery and turned on the phone. The screen brightened. *Good, I've got five bars; we're on the air,* he thought. He dialed 011 then his mom's cell phone number. Seconds later, it began to connect! It gave a tone. *Yes, yes, yes!* But before he heard his mom a robot message said, "Sorry, the number you have dialed has been disconnected."

Disconnected? Impossible! He thought. He tried his dad's cell phone number. Same thing—disconnected. He was still doing something wrong. *But what?* Then it hit him, *maybe the 011 prefix is for making calls to places outside the United States.* He decided to try the number on the card.

He punched in the numbers and waited. *Beep—beep—Ring! Ring! Ring!*

The call went live, and a voice said, "Hallo," followed by words in a language he couldn't understand.

"English, please! English please, I only speak English!" said Justin.

"How can I help you," said the voice in enunciated English.

"My name is Justin Cody. I am on a canoe trip in Canada. My grandpa is gone. I'm all alone. Please help me. I am on a satellite phone, but I don't know how to use it to call my mom. Please, will you call her for me if I give you the number?"

"Certainly," said the voice calmly, "what's the number?"

Justin gave the man his mom's cell phone number.

"Got it," said the friendly voice. "Tell me, Justin, do you know the number of your satellite phone?"

"No," replied Justin.

"Hmm. Okay, I'll call your mom. But you can call her yourself. From Canada, you need to first dial 001, then the area code, followed by your mom's number. Got it?"

"001. 001. Yes, yes! I got it. Thank you very much. Please call her for me now."

"Okay, I will. Good luck. Bye now."

Justin immediately tried to dial his mom, but he was so excited that his hands trembled, and he kept hitting the wrong numbers. When he finally got them right, the line was busy. He figured the man was talking to her now. He decided to wait awhile then try again. When he thought enough time had passed, he tried again.

His mom answered on the very first ring. "Justin? Justin, are you okay? Are you okay?" she asked in a frightened voice.

"Fine, Mom, I'm fine. Gramps is gone and I'm alone. Get me outta here, Mom! Get me outta here!"

"Okay, okay. Settle down. What do you mean Gramps is gone?" she asked with alarm.

"He's gone, Mom, I dunno. I'll tell you later. It'll be okay, he'll come back, I know it. Just get me outta here."

"Okay, okay. Where are you?"

"I'm camped on a big lake. It's called, umm, Otter Lake. I'm on the east side of it, real close to where the river flows out of the lake."

"Okay, honey," his mom responded. "I'll take care of it. I promise. Give me a few hours to figure this thing out, then call me back and I'll have details. Meanwhile, stay safe. I love you, Justin!"

"I know, Mom; me too."

"Bye now."

"Wait, wait, wait! Mom! Tell them to bring food—lots of food!"

"Of course, honey. Love you." The call ended with a click.

For several minutes, Justin just sat there, cross-legged on the ground, holding the phone and staring at it. He couldn't believe he had just talked to his mom and would soon be rescued. He slapped his face; he needed to prove it wasn't a dream.

He thought about the fit he'd had when Gramps tried to show him how to use the satellite phone. "I know how to use a damn phone!" came back to haunt him. *Stupid, stupid, stupid,* he scolded, *How could I have been so damn stupid?* If he had only listened, he would have been rescued weeks ago. When he had finished beating himself up, he stood up and did a little dance of relief. Then he stretched out his arms to the sky and loudly yelled, "Thank you, phone! Thank you!"

Justin noted the time of the call recorded on the phone. He planned to call his mom back in exactly two hours. To pass the time, he wrote in his journal. He was very hungry, but not for fish. His head was swimming with visions of burgers and pizza, ice cream and chocolate. Why bother to fish? He was getting!

Several times, he turned on the phone to check the time. When, to the minute, two hours had passed, he called his mom. She answered on

118

the first ring. She said there was good news and bad news. The good was that a float plane was coming to get him. The bad was that the air base was fogged in. If the fog lifted soon, the pilot would be there today. If not, it would be tomorrow, or whenever the weather cleared. She said that the pilot would call her when it was safe to fly.

"Okay, Mom, I understand," he said in a disappointed voice. Then he turned off the phone and put it away.

Justin turned his attention to building a signal fire—he didn't want the rescue plane to miss him! He was even more meticulous than before. When he had finished, he returned to the tarp to wait. He waited and waited. Twilight came, then darkness, and there was no sound of an airplane. Disappointed, he built up his campfire and went to bed, but he couldn't sleep and just laid there, eyes wide-open all night, ready to bolt out of bed at the break of dawn.

He awoke early, excited that the plane would come today, but when he saw sprawling fog covering the lake, he doubted that it would. There was nothing he could do but sit and wait and hope that the sky would clear soon. He started the fire and heated some water and then washed.

To kill time Justin decided to go fishing. Hours passed, and nothing happened. *Not a single strike? Come on!* Hungry and frustrated, he returned to camp and called his mom. She told him that the air base was still fogged in and that it didn't look like it would clear today. She assured him, though, that the pilot would leave as soon as he could see. Reluctantly, Justin said he understood.

For a long time after their talk, Justin just sat by the campfire and stared into the flames. He thought about how his mom was always there for him—sometimes so much so that she drove him crazy. She meant well, but she would often go ballistic when he tried adventurous things like climbing trees or swimming where there were no lifeguards. Once, he crashed his bike while both of his parents were watching. His mom screamed and had a fit while his dad just asked if he was okay. He loved his mom deeply, but he wished she'd lighten up and let him fly. He wondered if when he got home, would she still freak out when he did things that she thought were dangerous.

He also thought about school and how he was always getting into trouble for playing on his cell phone. He wondered why he had been so addicted to it. Was it the fun of texting and playing games, or was he just bored with school and needed to pass the time? Here, in the wilderness, he was never bored! There was just too much to do to be bored! He hadn't even thought about his cell phone or computer since Gramps left, and strangely, he didn't miss them at all, not even his favorite games.

Their vibrance had faded, replaced by something magical about the wilderness—the beauty of a sunrise, the soft breeze against his face, the sweet smell of cedar trees, the sound of waves crashing against a rocky beach, the thrill of catching huge fish and eating them for supper, the sight of a bear or wolverine. The wilderness made him feel alive and capable. He realized that as much as he wanted to go home, *wanted to be home,* part of him was sad to leave this place. He stirred the glowing coals with a stick then looked longingly into the thick fog. "Yep, Gramps, I think I have your genes," he mumbled through tears and a smile. Then he settled in for the night, with high hopes that the airplane would come tomorrow.

Just after daybreak—22 days after Gramps was spirited away— Justin heard the sound of an engine. The fog had lifted! He leapt out of bed and lit his signal fire. He dipped the green boughs in water so that they would smoke more fiercely. In the distance, he saw an airplane. It was flying low, circling the lake. It was turning, banked to the left, away from his camp, so the pilot couldn't see the smoke. Then it turned west and disappeared behind the islands.

Justin was stunned. *Didn't he see me?* He had a smoky fire going and he was jumping up and down and waving his arms. *How could the pilot have not seen me?!* Besides, he had told his mom exactly where he was. *What should I do! What should I do!* There was nothing he could do but wait and hope the plane would come back again and keep feeding the fire. He stoked it higher and higher with evergreen boughs. "Come back, plane, come back! Please come back!" he pleaded.

It wasn't long before the plane came back into view. It was coming straight towards camp! When it was only a couple hundred yards away, it powered down and the plane dropped gracefully onto the water, then chugged slowly towards him. Just before the pontoons touched shore, the pilot cut the engine and the plane silently drifted in. An elderly, gray-haired man who was wearing red suspenders was already standing on a pontoon. He jumped ashore, rope in hand, and tied the plane to a tree. Justin ran to the airplane.

"Gramps! Gramps! Gramps!" he called. "Is that really you?"

"Sure is, son!" he hollered back. "Oh my God, I'm so glad you're alive!"

Hugs and hugs and more hugs followed. Then food. There was a cooler filled with sandwiches, apples, potato chips, pop, and cookies. Justin wolfed down a PB & J. He couldn't remember when one had tasted so good. Gramps dug in too. Between bites, they excitedly shared some of their experiences, but more would come later when they got home and things settled down. Right now, they were just thrilled to find each other. While they were eating, Gramps reached into a pocket and pulled out a small wooden object.

"For you. It's a whistle—whittled it myself." He said with a smile.

Justin blushed and gave the whistle a tweet. "Thanks, Gramps," he said and gave Gramps another hug.

When they'd had their fill, they loaded up their stuff and helped the pilot tie on the canoe. They tied it to the left pontoon so that the pilot could watch it while he flew, that way, if a rope loosened up, he would see it. If it became a problem, he would land on the nearest lake and fix it.

Justin looked at the pilot—a trim, short man with a full mustache— and asked, "Has a canoe ever fallen off your airplane?"

"Just once, many years ago, when I first started flying. A big canoe like yours came untied and fell about 1,000 feet and landed in a swamp.

It was on the right pontoon-float, so I never saw it fall. We were lucky it didn't hit the airplane on its way down. If it had, I wouldn't be here flying you today."

"What happened to the canoe?" asked Justin.

"Broke a seat and the carrying yoke, that's all. Those Royalex canoes are tough." he replied.

"Yeah, ours went over a falls, but I fixed it and paddled it 30 miles to here," said Justin proudly.

"I heard the story! You're quite a kid, Justin. I think you'd make a great bush pilot someday." The pilot smiled.

"I think I wanna be a famous software engineer like my dad." Justin beamed.

"Good choice," said the pilot. "It pays better than this and it's a whole lot safer. And you won't be constantly swatting bugs." With this, he squished a mosquito against the windshield then started the engine.

A minute later, they were in the air—heading for a town that had warm beds and the kind of food Justin had been dreaming about for weeks. When Justin asked the pilot how he could have missed his smoky fire, the man replied that he saw four smokes coming in—one on a rocky point and a group of three, arranged in a triangle on a beach farther west. He flew to the three, thinking it was him. "I realized my mistake when I picked up your grandfather. Sorry you had to wait," he said with a smile.

As soon as they were in the air, the pilot handed Gramps his satellite phone. "Better call your daughter and tell her we got him!" A minute later, Justin's mom was on the phone and everyone was wet with tears of joy.

CHAPTER 21 — HOME

Justin's first week back at home was delightful but difficult. It was hard getting used to a new routine. He didn't have to catch fish or rabbits or birds or porcupines or collect fireweed leaves and blueberries. He could eat as much as he wanted whenever he wanted, and all he had to do to get it was to open the refrigerator door. Equally awesome were lights that shined with the flick of a switch, and water that flowed when you turned a knob.

It was wonderful to be home, but there was something odd about it. He wondered if it was the new "conveniences" he enjoyed, or the limits imposed by his mom. Maybe it was because civilization was less exciting than canoeing down a wilderness river. He recalled a comment by a friend who'd heard his story. "Welcome back to the hard life!" he said. Justin just smiled—his friend didn't have a clue how difficult it was to live outdoors.

He spent a lot of time with Gramps. They talked a lot about the canoe trip and how they had each managed to survive. They appeared on local radio and TV shows, and a reporter wrote a feature story about them for the local newspaper. They were questioned by the FBI, who later told them they were lucky to be alive—that they had found the plane and the aerodrone. Both were burned to a crisp! Suddenly, they were celebrities, and everyone wanted to hear about their trip.

Justin wanted to call Sara and tell her the news, but he wanted her to see the news about him before he called. He thought about mailing her a copy of the newspaper, care of her aunt, but he didn't know the address and he was too shy to call her parents and ask. Anyway, she would be home in time for school. He would call her then—or maybe, he'd wait until she called him!

The goofy part was that Justin had been home for nearly a week before he turned on his cell phone. Then he just checked his messages and put the phone aside. The dark, complex games he had loved to play before the canoe trip seemed less exciting now. His new interest was wilderness survival, and he was consumed with learning all he could about it. He was fascinated with stories about the great mountain men of the past—Daniel Boone, Kit Carson, Hugh Glass, Jim Bridger, John Colter, and more. Suddenly, he had become a "reader."

The rest of summer went fast, and school would be back soon. Strangely, Justin was excited to go. After all, he was famous now and he had an impressive tale to tell, and Sara would be there. A week before the opening day, Justin's mom got a call from the school counselor. The counselor said that Justin's 8th grade English and social studies teachers wanted to meet with him regarding their "alternative summer-school agreement." He said that Justin should bring his journal and some photos from the canoe trip. He asked Justin's parents to please attend—and said his grandpa was welcome too.

The meeting would take place a few days later, so Justin had plenty of time to prepare. He sorted his photos and loaded them onto his iPad so that everyone could easily see them. Before the canoe trip, he would have done anything to skip a meeting with his teachers. Anything! But this time, he'd done nothing wrong—in fact, he'd done everything right! He looked forward to the meeting, confident that his teachers would treat him well.

When Justin and his family walked in everyone rose and smiled. The counselor and then each of his teachers shook his hand. They patted him on the back, said nice things about him, and made him feel like a star. When he handed his journal to his English teacher, she smiled and politely asked if she could keep it for a few days—she promised to take good care of it. "Of course," replied Justin with an embarrassed grin. They all looked on excitedly as Justin showed his pictures of the trip. They nodded in disbelief at the hardships he'd endured. And everyone gasped when he showed the picture of the roasting porcupine!

When Justin had finished his presentation, the counselor asked if he would please step out in the hall for a few minutes, so they could discuss his fate. The counselor promised they wouldn't keep him long. A few minutes later, the door opened, and he was ushered in with smiles. His counselor declared, "Justin, we all agree that you have kept your part of the bargain—more than kept it—and so, we will keep ours. I'll let your teachers speak for themselves."

Justin's social studies teacher talked first. He said that the canoe trip was a life-changing experience—that no amount of schooling could equal what he had learned during that month on his own. He smiled and said, "Justin, I'm changing your *F* to a *C*. I'm really proud of you!"

Then his English teacher spoke, "I heard you on the radio, Justin, and I watched you on TV. You were literate and confident—exactly what we try to teach in language arts class. I'm giving you a *B*."

"I'd take an *A*?" Justin said with a grin.

"Don't push it," the teacher replied.

As they were leaving, his counselor asked Justin if he would do a presentation to the student body on the first day of school. "You don't have to if you don't want to," he qualified.

"Sure," said Justin, "I want to!"

CHAPTER 22 — SCHOOL DAZE

It was the night before the start of school, and Justin was excited. He had always hated school, but now, he couldn't wait to go. He had been up late thinking about his presentation. The entire middle school would be there—all of them, grades seven through nine. He was on pins-and-needles knowing that the audience would be so large. Most scary was that Sara would be there. He was sure she'd been home for a while and was sad she hadn't called. He wanted to call her. His mom said he should—that when she was a girl the boys called her; it was never the other way around!

"It's different now!" Justin defended his shyness.

His mom just grinned and countered, "If you're smart, you'll call her." He decided that he would—after the show!

Justin's presentation was scheduled for fifth period—meaning he had to endure four classes before he presented. But he sat through them all quietly and attentively, even though he was champing at the bit.

His classmates kept giving him admiring stares, as if to say, *We can't wait to see your show!* His teachers caught on immediately. They introduced him and praised him to the class. He loved the new attention, but he was embarrassed as much as he was proud. His face turned beet-red every time a teacher said his name.

Finally, the time arrived. The auditorium was packed—the entire school was there! Seeing so many kids sitting there, just to see him, encouraged him to do his best. And he did. When he finished, everyone clapped, then they stood up and clapped some more! The principal stood up and clapped too. Afterwards, the principal told Justin that he had received what was called a "standing ovation." "They loved your presentation!" he said enthusiastically.

As he was walking back to class, a dark-haired girl zoomed out of the shadows and ran up to him. It was Sara. She was practically shaking with excitement. "You're so cool, Justin, so cool!" she said quietly. Then she quickly kissed him on the cheek and ran off to class. "Call me when you get home," she called as she disappeared down the hall.

"I will! I will!" he answered back.

As he turned a corner, he saw his 8th grade English teacher standing in the hall. She came up to him and said she loved his presentation, and that after seeing it, she had changed her mind—and his grade—to an A. She also said his journal was fascinating and that one day he should write a book about his trip.

"What do you think you would call it if you did?" she asked.

Justin pondered, thinking deeply. Then he looked up brightly and replied, "RACE TO SURVIVAL!"

APPENDIX

APPENDIX 1: THREE KNOTS EVERYONE SHOULD KNOW

DOUBLE HALF-HITCH

Use two half-hitches to tie a rope to a tree. The knot won't slip or loosen. This is the knot that Gramps used to tie the canoe to a tree when it was on land. Additionally, the knot will release with a single pull if you run the free end back through the loop.

SHEET-BEND

Use this when you need to tie two ropes together. The knot will not slip, even when different diameter ropes are tied together. The knot must be made exactly as shown—that is, with both of the free ends on the same side. The knot will hold if they are on different sides, but it won't be as strong. If a thick rope and a thin rope are to be joined, the thin rope should be the "working" rope—that is, the one with which you make the knot. Tip: the knot will release instantly if you finish it with a "slippery loop."

Single sheet bend

Quick-release (slippery) half hitch. Pull to release.

BOWLINE

Use this when you want a very secure knot that won't slip under a load. Mountain climbers use this knot to tie their climbing ropes around their waists. It is an important rescue knot because it absolutely, positively will not slip. And it comes out easily, even after a load has been applied.

APPENDIX 2: TEN ESSENTIALS (PLUS, FOUR BONUS)

Always have these items with you when you go to the backcountry—even for just a few hours! Everything should fit into a small pack.

1. Map and compass: Topographic maps are best, but a simple road map can get you home alive. An Orienteering-style compass because it has a built-in protractor that helps you compute bearings off a map. Some also have built-in mirrors that can be useful for signaling.
2. Sunglasses and sunscreen for lips and skin.
3. Clothing for the season: a warm sweater, a waterproof jacket with a hood, and a hat. Clothing should be wool, nylon, polyester, or acrylic—no cotton!
4. A knife, preferably a multi-tool like Justin carried.
5. Strike-anywhere matches in a waterproof case and two butane lighters.
6. A waterproof fire-starter (trick candles, Vaseline-dipped cotton balls, waxed paper, etc.). Most paper absorbs moisture and is not a good fire-starter after time outside!
7. A small headlamp with fresh batteries.
8. A few first-aid items: Band-Aids, triple-antibiotic ointment, aspirin, a small roll of gauze, first-aid tape or duct tape, and water-purification tablets.
9. A water bottle.
10. A compact emergency shelter: tarp, space blanket, plastic tube tent, giant trash bags, small roll of duct tape.

You are also wise to carry:

11. A signaling device: whistle, cell phone, orange smoke grenade, bright laser pointer, signal mirror, etc.
12. Food: energy bars, nuts, dried fruit, jerky, etc.
13. Toilet paper.
14. Nylon parachute cord

APPENDIX 3: PEMMICAN YOU CAN MAKE AT HOME

There are many recipes for pemmican. Here's a simple one you can make at home:

INGREDIENTS:
1. One cup of dried meat: beef, bison, deer, or elk. You can dehydrate your own meat (best) or use "dried chipped beef," which is available in grocery stores. Pound the dried meat to a powder or cut it into very tiny pieces.
2. One cup of dried berries: blueberries, raspberries, mixed berries, etc.
3. One cup of animal fat: beef, bison, elk or deer. "Render" the fat, that is, cook it slowly and stir constantly so it doesn't burn. When the fat stops bubbling, the "rendering" is done. Use a metal strainer to remove all the little bits of meat. You just want the liquid.
4. Optional: Any or all-of the following: nuts, raisins, peanut butter, honey, maple syrup, salt and pepper. Important: adding wet ingredients like peanut butter, honey, etc. will shorten the shelf life of your pemmican!

PROCEDURE:
1. Put the ingredients into a bowl then pour the rendered fat over them. Add about one part of fat for every two parts of the other ingredients. Pour slowly—too much fat and you'll have runny pemmican! If your pemmican is too runny, you can thicken it by adding some almond meal (a "flour" made from almonds).
2. When the pemmican is firm, form it into squares or balls. Wrap the pieces in plastic wrap and store them in a cool, dry place. Put them in the freezer if you want to keep them for a very long time.

HOW DOES IT TASTE? If you're very hungry, it's great! Otherwise, you'll much prefer a burger!

APPENDIX 4: THREE IMPORTANT CANOEING STROKES

DRAW STROKE — Use this powerful stroke to turn the canoe.

Solo adaptation

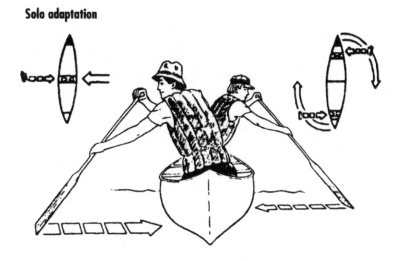

CROSS-DRAW STROKE — This is the opposite of the draw stroke. It turns the canoe away from your paddling side.

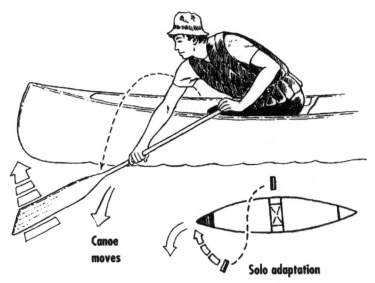

Canoe
moves

Solo adaptation

J-STROKE — Use this stroke to keep the canoe going straight, without changing paddle sides.

Start

Finish

Thumb of top hand is turned down.

To turn the canoe towards your paddle, add more "J" or "hook" at the end. When you are canoeing alone from the center of the canoe, the stroke will look more like the letter C than a J. Notice that the thumb of the top hand is turned down at the end of the stroke. That's the correct way to do it. But if you need more power, turn your thumb up at the end, then pry the paddle smartly away from the canoe.